I0710281

The Book Of Crow

Lyle Rexer

Drawings by Donald Alberti

SPUYTEN DUYVIL

New York City

Parts of this book appeared in a different form in the *Brooklyn Rail* and *New Observations 133: Real≠Reality*.

© 2024 Lyle Rexer
ISBN 978-1-963908-26-8

Library of Congress Control Number: 2024945882

For Rachel

In the American Museum of Natural History there are undiscoverable rooms. In one of them lived—better say worked or habitated—an amateur ornithologist. Volunteer research assistant was the title he adopted, and the rest of the department allowed that, as long as he brought coffee. Had it been anyplace else but the academic backwater of a natural history museum, such a thing would have been administratively excised. Here he was protected by institutional amnesia. No office, of course, but an alcove partially hidden. He surrounded himself with the amplified sounds of birds via an antique pair of Koss headphones and images via Kodachrome slides he salvaged after they had been digitized. He ran errands in the museum, a vast bulk whose innards no single person claimed to know. He tried working as a docent but was too entranced by the dioramas to talk. He studied migration maps and DNA sequencing results. For fun he drew strange cladistic trees, attempting to account for the branching of species after the great extinction event (Permian version). The names he repeated to himself were those of the naturalists Ray, Aldovrandi, and Lack; ornithologists Mayer, Streseman, Chapman, and Tinbergen. He once called raven expert Bernd Heinrich the greatest living novelist. On his museum ID card he substituted a picture of Charles Darwin. From time to time, he opened the specimen drawers just to admire the color of a Baltimore oriole. The vast majority of the birds he studied he had never seen in person, and some of them no longer existed as species. The ancient department secretary, who knew where everything was, watched out for him. He admired her sweetness and patience.

He dreamed of going to Papua New Guinea, to Colombia, to Darien on the isthmus, to the Hebrides. He pored over pictures of the migrations in the Tagus delta and the Platt River as if they were a kind of pornography. (It became a departmental joke.) They let him answer the nonscientific correspondence and emails because of his acerbic tongue. He enjoyed jousting with flat-earthers and anti-evolutionists, but even more the questions from the bird watchers, who always claimed to have seen species new to science. Over time he became obsessed with habitat destruction and blasted off more and more intemperate posts on X. The department secretary suggested that he might want to take a break.

He spent more and more time in nearby Central Park observing. He tracked certain birds into the Ramble and had to be directed out by a park ranger. He practiced bird calls from a phone app. He fantasized establishing a global office of avian surveillance, with real-time feeds from Malaysia to the Azores. He often did not go back to his apartment, but the department secretary never managed to discover where he slept (he didn't).

One day he didn't come in. And for weeks after that. The department secretary carefully went through the archaeological mound of his desk. She found a violently annotated copy of an old Peterson field guide to North American birds and the hand-written, occasionally illustrated manuscript printed below.

1. The Last of Crow

(for D. M. Campbell, M.D.)

Crow looked over a world he never made and found it not so bad, something he could live with if he had to.

Crow was not burdened with big ideas. He liked to say there were two kinds of creatures in the fields—those who stood still and those who couldn't stop moving. He likened them to the difference between strategists and tacticians. Crow was strategic, but impulsive.

Crow's friends sometimes asked him about the past. For some reason, they loved post-egg reminiscences: the trauma of first flight (some schadenfreude here as they related stories about birds that hadn't learned to fly and failed—fatally—their first and only test); being fed in the nest and the reassurance of that beak-to-beak contact; the coital triumphs based on their plumage displays. ("My colors were out of sight, super fresh, and I totally smashed them, but no, we're not still together.") They were all so gregarious. It was like a locker room. Crow said: "I remember wet warmth, a time before sunlight and the amazing appearance of feathers. I remember my saurian ancestors." That put a stop to conversation.

Flying, Crow thought: What was the proper height for his kind? High enough to see the Earth's near edge but not so high that he lost sight of burnished rooftops, the fenceposts and wire that stitched the land together, the intricate tangle of forests, so much like the hair of human beings, the sinuous bend of a river when its surface catches the sun. Leave the upper atmosphere to the raptorial birds, the hunters who drop like stones toward their prey. That was an extreme sport he never had a taste for. But he could imagine it.

And speaking of death, Crow opened his eyes each morning on a mountain of corpses—all part of the world as he found it. He was used to coming last and wasn't insulted by the reputation; *l'ultimo viene il corvo* they said in Italy. But he preferred the French: *Après le deluge, moi.* It sounded grander, more important, the triumph of the survivors. Whatever. He thought of himself as a realist, and that set him apart from birds that dove and dropped and dug to get their food. They had appetites. Crow had tastes, because he did not kill, he curated, he chose. He stayed away from the shrikes, torturers. Something went so wrong with them; there was no discussion. But he hated the vultures. They were addicted to carrion, in love with death, and it warped them. You could see it in their eyes. (Clearly, Crow was feeling defensive about his own habits.)

Crow's dreams often involved other animals, other ways of being. Visions of the peewit, the crocodile, the boa constrictor came to him often. Once he dreamed he was a wolf. The dream went like this: He was flying through the woods, where he almost never went, and saw a wolf in the distance. It looked like the farmer's dog, scrawny brown and silver but still as a piece of wood. When Crow approached on gigantic wings, the animal sprang into the air. Crow felt himself lifting off powerful hind legs, touching down here and there, zigzagging like a deer, and moving among the maze of trees at a speed more thrilling than flight.

Crow referred to his nest as the Bat Cave and rarely let anyone inside. With good reason. They couldn't handle it. They would be like Marco Polo at Khan's court, refusing to believe that such a place could exist outside their very limited belief systems and financial arrangements. They would be dazed by the bottle caps, shards of glass, tarnished necklaces, tinfoil, quahog shells burnished like pearl, and even a wristwatch, whose sound Crow imitated and fell asleep to. The watch died, and Crow had to content himself with turning it over to look at the inscription whenever he felt that things couldn't get worse: "Presented by President Dwight D. Eisenhower for faithful service." The wealth would be incomprehensible to them, the sight of it sure to blind them or drive them crazy with envy. He didn't want their blindness on his conscience. (In secret, they laughed at him. "Have you been in Crow's crib? Utter trash, man. The dude has absolutely no taste. And he needs a clutter consultant.")

Crow knew many things, but he didn't know one thing.

Because he was attracted to mirrors, Crow often contemplated his appearance, which led him to consider the negritude of certain birds. Ravens, grackles, starlings, various ducks, loons, blackbirds. He asked himself what they all had in common except an acquaintance with the night. At the moment of their origin, there would have been no moon, and night must have been so thick and excessive it rubbed off on all of them and spread throughout the world. Blackness is night's protection against the sun, against the moon. Might there be planets where the crows were white, arctic planets ruled by owls?

In the field stood what they laughingly called a scarecrow. It didn't scare anyone, and the crows loved to play hide and seek with it. Crow perched on the shoulder of the simulacrum and used this blank interlocutor to practice his language skills. To be among the tongues of men and not to know them seemed to him an intolerable prohibition. But human speech was infinite, variable, chaotic. Crow tried to remember all that he had heard and repeat it back: "The universe in a grain of sand." Caw. "Ask not what you can do for your country." Caw. "A whop bop-a-lu bop, a whop bam boom. Tutti frutti." Caw. "History is a nightmare from which I am trying to awake." Caw caw caw. The scarecrow did not have to say anything about how ridiculous it all sounded. His silence was devastating. Crow croaked at him, "What have you accomplished with all your fine words? You don't scare anybody. You just know how to curse a little better, that's all."

Crow didn't know about the ghosts until he lit on a windowsill to get out of the rain and looked inside the room on the other side of the glass. The only light came from the television, turning the family into mere silhouettes. Out of the glowing square poured the images—people talking, laughing, car chases, disasters, a triple double for Lebron, with his brow like a hunk of kneaded putty, the Wheel of Fortune. The pictures filled the room, pushed through the glass and crowded around Crow. There were so many of them, and they just kept coming. He felt he was going to suffocate, but they dissipated into thin air. Where did they go? Crow asked obsessively. Have you seen them?

Crow slept less and less. Awake, he practiced extreme vigilance. He felt that everything depended on this. Take it easy, Crow, you're wrapped too tight. That was the common assessment.

Crow caught sight of himself in the white enameled surface

of a gas pump: hollow-eyed, heavy, aging badly. No wonder they mistook his yellow pupils for nicotine poisoning. A waxwing flew by, sharply dressed—unnecessarily, in Crow's opinion. "Crow, man, what happened to you? You totally let yourself go."

Crow saw more and more. He saw the roots of plants burrowing like blind bulbs in the thick soil darkness. He saw water cutting new channels through the soil. He saw forests burning in blossoms of light. He saw the surface of Earth shift and open, swallowing whole cities. He saw doctors running off to other emergencies. He saw a prisoner tying shoelaces into a noose. He saw a woman dreaming of sculptural perfection. He saw ice losing its grip. He saw a library of books whose black letters were meant only for him, letters he could almost read. He saw the forms of everything change in a universe without essences. Anything might become anything, given enough time.

Crow's short neck had always prevented him from looking up. No birds he knew had ever looked up, but now he could. The sky was open to him. He looked up and understood that the answer to his unasked questions was there above his head. It had been there the whole time, scattered like salt on a table, glittering like the glass he hoarded in his nest, its brightness glimpsed only in a reflection he once saw on a winter lake. The stars had their own velocity; Crow could barely tell they were moving, but he could tell. Maybe it came at the right time, the message. The stars said: You need to quit thinking of trees. You need to stop looking for a green that doesn't exist. You need to be patient and live.

2. Crow in Two Inadequate Descriptive Systems

System 1

Corvidae (that is, *Corvus albus* up to and including *Corvus woodfordi*)

Crow's nest

Crow's feet

Eat crow

Old Crow

Scarecrow (as if!)

Counting crows

Crow-magnon

Crowbar (noun)

Crowbar (verb: "He crowbarred the box open")

Crowbar (another sort of bar)

As the crow flies

A murder of crows

Jim Crow

Russell Crow(e)

Cameron Crow(e)

Sheryl Crow

Jose Cuervo

Chief Fool's Crow

Orville Crow, Jr. (aka Newton Thornburg)

Crow over

Crow about

Up with the crows

Stone the Crows

The Black Crows
As the crow flies (or has to walk and roll a flat tire)
Carrion crow
Ungwish-wungwa
Crow nation

SYSTEM 2

The crow wished everything was black, the owl that everything was white.

By dropping golden beads near a snake, a crow once managed to have a passerby kill the snake for the beads.

The Veneti may have been stupid, but they were also Italian, so when the crows were destroying their harvest, they decided to take a shortcut and bribe them. Two thousand years later, crows in Venice still expect a handout.

Better a short-lived celestial swan than a century-lived crow.

A crow will not pull out the eye of another crow.

Nothing is unreal as long as you can imagine like a crow.

Offer a crow a handshake, and all you'll get is a claw.

The eagle never lost so much time as when he submitted to learn of the crow. (Amen to that, amen.)

The one thing you know as a crow is that you are going to have to get your feathers dirty.

Crow was rainbow colored, feathers flashing like a kaleidoscope. He could sing like Caruso, like Jessye Norman and Bette Midler. But it hardly mattered. The Earth was cold and the air colder. Crow asked available deities for warmth, and they all said the same thing: What's done is done, and the universe can't be undone. But one of them stuck a rolled-up newspaper into the sun, where it burst into flame, then threw it into the cosmic void, also known as the night sky. Crow caught it; it was on fire! As a matter of fact, it was fire, the essence of fire. Crow's wings turned black with smoke, and his voice cracked and failed. I'll never get this stuff off, he thought, and my voice is shot. He didn't, and it was. But the Earth was warm thereafter, and creatures everywhere cut him a lot of slack. Sometimes, if the sun is right, you can see flashes of the brilliance he once wore, she once wore, they once wore.

Utnapishtim sent a dove and a crow to find land after the deluge. Guess which one came back? Guess which one found land and didn't bother to come back to tell anybody else about it?

A crow and an eagle went hunting. The eagle could do whatever it wanted. It attacked with talons and beak because it feared nothing and no one and everyone knew the rules. But the animals scattered after one strike, one victim, one scapegoat, and it had to go hunting again, and this time the animals were somewhat more prepared. The crow watched in admiration but without envy. There was already plenty of killing. There was already plenty to eat.

The Sioux leader Little Crow led a brief rebellion in Minnesota during the Civil War, which was put down. Several years later, a white farmer shot Little Crow when he happened on him picking blackberries. The farmer beheaded Little Crow and skinned him. The Minnesota Historical Society had the skin for some time. Not only native people but it is quite possible crows, too, have never forgotten this outrage.

It's too late for the dead to notice, but the crow always comes last.

3. Crow in the Time of Cholera

Crow came back to the city. It took him a while. Once burned, as they say. He said to himself, They hear what they want to hear, see what they want to see, pretend nothing happened. And yet, I think I can handle it. The problem was, Crow remembered. In truth, Crow remembered everything. No one he knew paid attention to anything he or they themselves said, but for some reason, Crow felt compelled to hold them to it, every last claim or boast or soon to be abandoned position. To remind them. I mean, who listens? Is that a crime? Crow, you can be such an asshole sometimes.

Crow felt he was the last of this kind, cursed with memory. He remembered how suddenly and completely everyone he knew had vanished from the streets and skies. He thought of it that way rather than "died" or were wiped out. Some avian flu or West Nile or who knew what. It was mostly rumor, but the devastation was real. He didn't use the word holocaust. It had been a black city, elegant, formal, wised up. But Crow saw his friends drop from the sky, pitch out of their nests, disappear into thickets with the instinct of the damned. Crow shunned their places of congregation, harmless pleasures after all but harmless no longer, to sit on a wire or gather in the tall trees of the park to make fun of the various animal populations and generally stir things up. Crows eyed each other suspiciously, always with the unspoken question: Are you sick? And the corollary: How do I know I'm not? The answer to both was not long in coming. The most beautiful and flamboyant were the first to disappear.

They seemed so frivolous once, but now Crow felt utter despair at their absence.

He grew weary of reciting the names of friends gone, but he did it as a form of exorcism, or penance: Heckel (with his put-on Brooklyn accent), Jeckel, EAPoe (who loved to pretend he was a raven), Jim Crow, Old Crow, Morgan Freeman, Tedford Hughes, Joe Cuervo, Gillo Pontecorvo, the list went on and on. Once he took a feather from a dead bird's wing, risked infection, and kept it.

Crow went out only at night. He avoided everyone and those old pleasures, not out of fear but out of a sudden sense of dignity. Any intimate act was unthinkable. Thwarted nature was a phrase he repeated. He put by shiny things. He cursed his own failures and every insignificant or false word he had ever spoken.

At the time, it was infuriating that so many were untouched and oblivious. Crows are not invisible! became a sort of battle cry. He would harangue heedless orioles, combative jays, even hummingbirds—they had the attention span of a gnat. "Don't you see what's happening? These are birds just like you!" He just wanted to shake them the fuck up, banish the sweetness of their lives with the taste of affliction.

Good luck with that. A tree full of sparrows chirped, "It's not our fight." And, "You must have had it coming."

At his low point, Crow felt that living in the city he belonged to the living dead. He recited a poem he heard somewhere that fit his sepulchral mood:

Take nothing,
put it inside nothing,
add nothing to it,
and to prove it doesn't exist,
squash it flat as nothing with nothing…

It sounded like a lullaby, but Crow did not let it hush him to sleep. He refused to lie cataleptic. He picked a fight with a hawk in Prospect Park. When disease hit the streets, they generally kept away. Empty environmental niches weren't good for them. But this one's equanimity pissed Crow off. It could have ended very badly, which was exactly what Crow wanted. Suicide by bird. But the hawk put a talon on Crow's neck and looked down at him like Mister T, like he was a pitiful fool. "Hasn't anybody talked to you about survivor's guilt?" he asked.

Crow left the city, never to return, he thought.

Crow came back.

He answered questions with the phrase "upstate." (That wasn't strictly accurate. He spent the entire time, however long it was, between Gurney's Inn and the Montauk Lighthouse. He might have been there for the duration, a beautiful empty stretch of grass and dune, and every morning it was like the light touched there first of all places in the world. But one day he decided to cruise Bridgehampton, and when he came back, the beach was leveled, and the McMansion was half up. The next lot was already marked out. He had no choice but to move on, and the city might be the only place where he could sustain disappointment. He knew it.)

This time, he was determined to keep his eyes open. Shy away from nothing. Yes, he felt the loneliness of knowing no one and being known by no one. True invisibility. But to savor anything, you must be a stranger to it. The places to roost, he had forgotten how thrilling they could be. He sat on a window ledge on the twenty-fourth floor of the Chrysler building and felt the sun descend the building's skin in the early morning. He bore witness to light on the water from the wing of an X-15 on the deck of the *Intrepid*. Traffic flowed along Broadway like a molten river, and he followed it until he was exhausted, came to rest on the statue of Christopher Columbus. The park was woven of green and brown beyond the limit of his sight. Who needed the Matterhorn, the Eiger, or K-2? (Were there crows in Tibet? He wasn't at all sure. Definitely in China.) He ascended straight up along the face of the Freedom Tower until the air began to thin and the currents no longer sustained him. He needed bigger wings! Infinitely wide, so that he could float as if he were nothing, all mind, one with that force that scarcely noticed cities and taunted them with fierce weather. Crow could see it all; he knew how everything worked. He heard the infrastructure complain and sensed the real estate deals being made. Whenever we are in the city, he thought, we want a bigger city.

At last, Crow, the damaged one, had everything, needed no one. The sun burned his wings, melted their waxy blackness. Careful Crow! A bird, too, can fall like Icarus, in a cloud of feathers, or burn like the phoenix into nothing and myth.

Crow carried the memory of this pure transparency with him.

4. Crow Versus the Grand Ennui

Crow was overland touring in his new Ferrari at just about a hundred and some. He was returning home from an avian party where he got a little drunk on gin. As the headlights cast a glow on the road, he heard a voice inside his head. It said, "You lost the light, now you're flying through the night, flying from the Grand Ennui."

To be truthful, there was no Ferrari, Crow obviously did not drive or consume alcohol (except once, accidentally, in the parking lot of Beverly Soon's Tofu Restaurant in Los Angeles, an experience better forgotten), nor did he often hear moral sanctions from an inner voice, which he also lacked. But he knew something about ennui. First of all, that it was a category of experience made up by left-leaning sociologists to describe or explain a complex set of feelings that ranged from mild but constant boredom to suicidal depression. Second, that its cause, source, foundation, and origin was the deracinated individualism of a capitalist system that substituted commodities for meaning and connection. Or maybe that was anomie he was thinking of. Yeah, that was it, anomie. Ennui was just boredom, the kind of thing most birds would feel if they thought about their own lives for more than a nanosecond, if they didn't live in the fool's paradise of an eternal present. Imagine the horror of living like that, starting every day over again just like the day before, and having absolutely no sense that you had done it all before, exactly the same way. But that lack of memory was what would make it bearable, possible, even liberating! Every day a new day! Every worm a new worm, every fuck the first fuck.

But just let someone outside that bubble make a comment like "Yesterday the bugs around here were so much better," and the bubble would explode. It would all come crashing down in the sudden recognition of being trapped by iron laws of biology.

That was not Crow's problem. He thought boredom was kind of funny, and that any place in which he was not bored was a place from which he had nothing to learn. But there were different types, with different implications, different textures. There was, for instance, the boredom of the desert. Not much to see and do, but details emerge with great precision and subtlety, a vocabulary of unsuspected distinctions, forty-seven words for the color brown. At the apex of day, your shadow measures only itself, and you feel doubled in a cosmic mirror. Flying over the desert, you see that shadow perfectly etched on the ground, moving with you, a fluid dark cross, a terrestrial you, you symbolized. At night, the temperature changes as swiftly as an eye closing. Crow was no connoisseur of landscapes, but the minimalism seemed to be imprinted deep inside him. So the desert induced a certain kind of boredom that provoked not dread but memory. Almost therapeutic. In the desert, you can see trouble from a long way off, provided you keep out of the declivities.

A couple of downsides, however. Sand is the reply to unasked questions, sand whose grains have no limit. What had he ever done in the desert except continually call himself into question by examining everything around him, down to the buzzing of a fly? Was it a fly, or some other winged and zinging insect? He wasn't even sure of that. Worried about becoming a wandering creature, Crow closed his eyes and refused to go on. What am I but a handful of fine sand lifted from the desert one day, carried a few steps, then scattered?

Less edifying was the crushing boredom of avian assemblies, the parliament of fowls that, no matter where he went, Crow felt he could not avoid. Crow was not a joiner, but he did not have enough feathers on his wings to count the times he had been sucked into the conversations of complaint that took place on light poles, tree branches, telephone lines, fences, roof peaks, seashores. Robins with their genocidal memories and biotech paranoia, unable to say anything but "Beware!" and "Never again!" The maddening placidity of pigeons, no not placidity, sang-froid: "The trouble with all of you is that you fail to appreciate the city. Cities are the future. Cities are the place where you can really take advantage of services, especially if you are older." Weaver birds struck him as nothing but social glad-handers. No matter what the topic, it was always, "Great to see you again. You look good, you look well. How about we all agree to disagree?" So it went, like a vast dictionary of received opinions and rote gestures. Macaws were okay, even though they tended to keep close and on the same page. When it came to habitat destruction, they knew chapter and verse and always had updated info. Politically speaking, Crow depended on them to keep him plugged in to the Issues, with a capital I. But he preferred to hang out with the sandpipers, plovers, and super chill phalaropes. Still, even that got old: "Crow, dude, you need to get some flip-flops, dig some coquinas, watch the sunset. This could be the right spot for you." Watching them all scuttle back and forth driven by the diurnal rhythms of the tide made him vaguely seasick.

The boredom of summer and bright colors. The boredom of waiting. The boredom of enforced isolation—remember the avian flu quarantine? The boredom of hobbies, mercifully avoided since Crow never had a job or took a vacation. The boredom of foreplay, mutually engaged. The boredom of hospital architecture and midwestern cemeteries. The boredom of weather: Why only four seasons? The boredom of the great sea, surging and yearning, sometimes crimson like fire. The boredom of entropy, with everything always, always tending to shit. The boredom of the heavens and the unassailable starry curtain. The boredom of Crow's own boredom, become the least interesting thing in the world.

If only there were the equivalent of Ferraris or Omega watches or countesses with jeweled hands. If only there were deep, elaborate dreams to mitigate the constant presence of being, something really to look forward to, to wake up from still trailing the remnants like smoke from a forest fire. To know the reality of two worlds. Instead, it was mostly fish, flesh, and rotting food. Crow envied human beings only this, nothing else, the complexity of their dreams. Dreams that nourished everything he did not have: fantasy objects, deep desires, morbid fears, the liberating power of transgressive violence.

Instead, Crow had the thin satisfaction of an ego, knowing who and what he was. Enough, Crow, stop beating yourself up (which is really boring).

Remember that some take devious credit for virtues they don't have by magnifying their own shortcomings. Some assume the guilt in order to take credit for the crime. Which is, after all, a better definition of ennui.

5. Crow Meets Mr. Bones
(in memory of John Berryman)

Crow was feeling depreciated, like old office furniture. Crow suspected that somehow a bell had been hung on his neck with the purpose of scaring away friends and females. His dreams yielded little in the way of premonitory insight. At best they were like the dream of the talking dog. The dreamer approached the beast until it could almost whisper in his ear. He heard only nonsense. Too late he realized that even in a dream, it is never important what the dog says but only that the dog can talk at all.

In the face of depression, he resorted to his usual evasive strategy that therapists had been calling him out about forever: He took flight, going nowhere in particular. You might actually make some progress if you were just willing to do the emotional work, they told him. Instead, you book a trip to Paris or wherever and throw your treatment out the window just when things are getting the most interesting. I am tempted, Crow, to publish my notes about our sessions just so everyone can see the mass of truth and falsehood tied up together in one bird brain.

But therapy presumes you have an interest in yourself, a huge interest. Crow had no such interest. He was bored with himself, "heavy bored." He landed on the railing of a high bridge. Below him was the usual abyss and, at bottom, the great river. At the other end of the bridge, he saw a short man in a trench coat with the beard of a Hassid. An apparently nonsensical line came to mind: The overcoat has all the jokes. Something about the hunched and rumpled nature of the coat suggested that under it there might be wings. A bird such as Crow had never seen, or an angel? Crow approached, warily. When he finally came within hailing distance, the man nodded. His eyes were red. He said: "I used to have a beautiful singing voice. Once in a sycamore I was glad, all at the top, and I sang. I could sing anything, even if I heard it only once. I could sing *Stella by Starlight*. Now I sound like you."

Crow ignored the insult because it seemed to him that here, at last, was someone he could talk to, someone who also knew "the song a robin sings/ through years of endless springs," even if he didn't sound like Ella. Someone to pay attention to if only because Crow heard that song so rarely. But with that, the man took off his trench coat and laid it on the railing. No wings were concealed, just the man alone, who had lost his voice. He removed his glasses and put them on the ground. He climbed over the railing, waved at Crow, and dropped into the void like a swan.

Crow followed him almost all the way down.

6. Crow Demurs

There were a number of things that Crow disliked, beyond the usual threats. Annoyances, he would call them, or something more complicated, having to do with being born into a world he never made and would not necessarily have chosen. He had a habit of listing them, but putting them in categories or even in some rank order was a job for the emperor's encyclopedists:

Turks and Caicos

Fallout shelters

Flaubert's parrot

The future

Accidents at railroad crossings

Mission oak

Strangler figs

Wislawa Syzymborska, out of jealousy, though Crow was rarely jealous of humans

Masahisa Fukase, out of envy for his love of ravens

London, Ontario

Twitter

Strychnine, because of the collateral damage

DDT, ditto

Home telescopes

The Stage

The Cinema

Martial arts, jiu-jitsu in particular

BB guns, especially the Daisy carbine

Coupons, rebates, cash back

Options, as in "What are my options?"

Options, as in "I'll take an option." (Crow had no financial instruments and was unlikely to acquire any.)

The Riddle of Identity

The Riddle of Age

The Riddle of Youth

Riddles of any kind, including enigmas, mysteries, *rompecabezas*, and anagrams

Jimson weed

Komodo dragons

Obsolescence

Novelty

The starry firmament

Catch and release

Beverly Soon's Tofu Restaurant (bad experience in the parking lot, mistaking a puddle for water)

Gin, tequila, and all other clear spirits (see previous example)

Colored electrical tape

Slinkies and fake barf (partial toward whoopee cushions)

Kayaks

Dead skunks in the middle of the road, stinking to high heaven

Bicycles (in Amsterdam)

The 90s

Time shares in Aruba and Park City

Wrens, because they suffer from body dysmorphia

Pelicans, because they don't

Montevideo, for its failure to halt bank robberies

The devil's right hand

Remoras

Creatives

The five of clubs

Figures of spiritual authority

The Cloud (as opposed to clouds)

Wasabi

Fate, as a concept

Out-of-pocket, as a misused expression

Sustainability

Clear cutting

Jobs that require new friends

The habit of looking down on oneself as if from a great height

Rejoice, O reason, Crow thought, for instinct can err, too.

7. Crow the Plumed Serpent: The Teachings of Don J

Nevertheless, Crow dreamt. And in contrast to the usual unbidden images, this one was harder to dismiss. He was trying to fly, but he had no wings. Coming down was the hardest thing. He plummeted and slowed to a crawl an inch above the ground, suspended in his own terror seemingly forever. When Crow woke up, it was into a gray and unconvincing world that took an entire day to regain its color.

Crow didn't buy the notion that dreams were premonitory. Just like he never believed that any animal—none he'd ever met—had powers of divination. What he knew about the future was: 1) the next meal; 2) the next fuck, which he never saw coming until he was on top of it—probably a good thing; 3) bad weather. His own time horizon was maybe a couple of days in either direction, longer than some but not by much and way shorter than many. On the other hand, he tended not to look back or second-guess even bad decisions. Still, the dream trailed him, and he wanted to understand it.

One day he heard about somebody in the Bronx, an old crow or some other avian kind, the sparrow who told him wasn't sure, but she thought he might be able to interpret such unconscious, upwelling imagery, though it sounded to her like garden variety loss-of-power anxiety. Any recent trouble with the plumbing as manifested in embarrassing and unsuccessful assignations? she asked. The sparrow acknowledged that Crow hadn't asked for her opinion. Fine. Crow could find the bird roosting in St.

Mary's Park in the Bronx. "He doesn't look like much, but he's got surprises, like tricks he plays on you, mind games kind of thing, and he does know mad shit about dreams." It seemed important for Crow's peace of mind to find this old crow or whatever, who could help him understand the terrible fear of falling and never touching the ground.

The park was way bigger than he expected. He asked around a bunch of pigeons hanging out on Cypress Ave. There were language issues, so he wasn't sure what he heard except that it seemed that this character wasn't a crow at all but a Yucatan jay. "Eh, you have to address him as *don*, he's old school." Yet Crow knew immediately who it was as soon as he saw him because he was so impossibly unlike anyone Crow would ever take seriously for any purpose. This bird was wizened, and his color was gone except for a trace of blue on his wings. His whole body was shriveled as if it had been in an oven. Desiccated. One of his eyes was rheumy and had a cataract as thick as a chicken claw. The other winked incessantly. The bird tottered on the limb like a drunk but never slipped off. Crow circled for a while before landing and then simply sat at a distance, pretending to be there for something else. After a long time, the other spoke: "Bring me some *aguacate*." It wasn't exactly speech. Crow didn't think anyone else could hear it except him: *aguacate*. Maybe just go with it and see what happens.

Crow was going to steal a small avocado from a bodega on 143rd street, but it wasn't necessary. Sitting on a bench as if it were left for him was the pitted fruit. He managed to carry the whole thing at once back to St. Mary's Park. The old jay said nothing but ate with a smacking sound—only after gesturing over each piece with his wing. Crow watched with diminishing curiosity as the bird ate the whole thing and burped. "That dream, didn't you notice me in it?" Again, words in Crow's head while the jay remained impassive. "Maybe next time," he heard, but Don J seemed to be asleep. How about never, thought Crow.

Two nights later he awoke in the same freefall. This is no dream, thought Crow, this is real! The fear surrounded him, moved around him like a pool or a tide. In the distance below, Crow could see something, a smudge of blue. As he hurtled toward it, the blue wave got bigger and bigger, filling the space of his dream, blotting out the sense of velocity. He couldn't tell if this blue wave was going to save him or smother him. He was at the edge of something fearful and thrilling, the instant of final transformation. Was it death, or some other state? He heard laughter somewhere.

The next day he found the jay in the same spot. He thought to say something about the dream, but Don J was busy arranging some things from his nest, apparently pieces of grass. Crow could also hear him singing. "B-b-b-b-bird bird bird, well the bird is a word. Don't you know about the bird? Well, everybody knows that the bird is a word." With that, he eyed Crow and took off. Crow followed without hesitation.

The jay flew with ease, into and out of the trees in the park, at times rising high above the neighborhood to survey its crowded streets, then diving and turning like an acrobat. Crow could barely keep him in sight, much less keep up. What the fuck! How old did they say he was? The jay landed on a metal scarecrow in a vest-pocket garden, a local place holder until the real estate sharks moved in. The don looked at Crow with his rheumy eye, and Crow heard the words, *"Hay que mostrar respeto a los espiritus de las plantas."* With that, he gave signs for Crow to pluck specific leaves from the kale, to pick unripe berries from the blueberry stems, and to dig up a baby arugula plant by the roots. The don is a trendy vegan chef, thought Crow as he carried the mess back to the park. Along with the bits of grass the jay had already accumulated, the plants formed a heap in the crook of the tree. "Don J, pardon my asking, but—"

The jay showed Crow his blue back. "It's going to rain, come back when the sun is out."

The night storm shook Crow's nest. He wondered if there weren't some kind of alternative to this constant exposure. He was pretty sure he had had that thought many times and always came to the conclusion that it could be worse. But it got him thinking: If you could make perfectly accurate predictions without fail, didn't that mean your thoughts were tied to events? So which came first? Quite possibly the thoughts. Like magic. The morning was stunning, and he got his ass up to the Bronx *cuanto antes.*

Don J was not yet awake, but next to him the roots, leaves, and vegetable whatnot had been carefully pecked into neat pieces and piled up to bake in the sun. Crow sidled up and poked it with his beak. A truly terrible smell wafted up and instantly filled Crow's head with fumes strong enough to make him vomit.

Don J opened one eye. "You don't eat the herb, you rub it on your wings, *pendejo*, otherwise her power will be too strong for you, and you will surely die. But if you follow my instructions the herb will take you to the place of your dream and answer your question."

Crow looked at the bird, who seemed to be laughing at him. "I'm not looking for a new religion. Can't we be more direct and you just deliver your sage advice? These dreams are really eating into my sleep time." Crow noticed he was standing in the pile of herb and his feet felt strangely numb. Don J suddenly reached out a wing and batted at the pile. Crow found himself covered with vegetable powder. Don J stared at Crow for a minute and then simply blew him a kiss. It felt like a whirlwind and knocked him off the branch.

Crow was falling like a stone! His wings wouldn't work; they windmilled like sticks. They were sticks, long and bony and sprouting what? His legs flailed as he fell faster, and the ground rose up like a wave. Crow's head was down bulleting toward impact. It was all happening again! The powerlessness come true. He instinctively put out his hands to brace the fall. Hands? He tucked his head in and grabbed his knees. Knees? Like an insect he curled into a ball, and his speed slowed at the last instant as he rolled lightly over the lawn of the park. He picked himself up, looked at himself, and saw legs, hands, feet, genitals, all misshapen and gigantic. There he stood, naked, without wings but wearing a tuft of feathers. Earthbound. A human being, or something plumed. The falling was his moment of transformation, his portal to a new world, like a flying shaman. He could hear Don J laughing. The herb will guide you. Hippie shit.

He walked, not knowing how. He was heavy on the ground,

and he could hear it tremble. With presbyopic eyes and the vision of an animal, he was sure he would bump into something, but the colors all around him were vivid and the heat of the sun spread over him like butter. He reached out with many-fingered hands, felt the pleasure of senses free from mere utility.

Birds circled and acted as if they didn't know him. He was not one of them any longer, despite his resplendent plumage, and their lives seemed so small and indistinct. He could see distant things. He could see near and tiny things. The colors dazzled him—azure, golden beryl, aquamarine. He could not fly, only cover the ground in leaps and long strides. This is what a god must feel like, he thought, but he had no concept for god, only the word.

Up ahead, he saw a pyramid had been raised, of money or lottery tickets or betting stubs. At the top someone in a feathered headdress just like his was waiting, a human painted ochre, red, and lapis, holding an obsidian knife. Was Crow transformed only to become a sacrifice? When he managed to get up the steep, crumbling steps to the top, the man-bird was gone. He could hear voices but see no one, voices speaking without words, a click language, a counting language. The clicking tallied time and delivered prophecy, warnings, intimations of world reversals and imminent collapse. He could understand every tap of the tongue, and he was the one who was making the sounds. They were his prophecies. There was no one else, only him, the supreme, the lowest raised up. When the world ended, he would end with it. In twelve thousand years. And the cycle would begin again. Don J was laughing somewhere, a giant vulture in the sky.

Crow threw up. Out came jewels with too many facets to count. Crow held them up to catch the sunlight. They reflected a jungled peninsula of smoking mirrors. Crow passed out.

He came to astride the limb of Don J's tree. He felt like he had been run over by a backhoe, worse than that time in the parking lot of Beverly Soon's Tofu Restaurant. "Did I travel, Don J?"

"A stupid question."

"But I'm here, right where I started. Did I physically travel? Did I fall?"

"Haven't you been somewhere? Why ask me? Who is anyone but you to say whether you traveled or how far you fell?"

"I'm pretty sure I was a Mayan king. You laughed at me in my dream."

"It was not in your dream that I laughed."

"Why did you laugh at me, Don J? Because I became a human being?"

"Or because you still think you are a crow?"

But a crow of a different kind. Crow was suddenly overwhelmed with nostalgia for the bird he had been. Now he knew abjectness and power, fear and delusional omnipotence, the certainty of destruction and the temerity of survival. There was no returning to a state he now regarded like a foreign country. He felt a sense of utter singularity in the face of his own life, now no longer his.

Well, you asked for it Crow. That is the cost of curiosity, that is the risk of a quest for vision. That was Don J's *chiste*, a shaman's joke that would never be something to laugh at but was the funniest thing in the universe Your world doesn't end in twelve thousand years, Crow. It ends in the moment of revelation that you are no longer what you thought you were, and nothing is as you thought it was.

He set forth to embrace this loss as if it were the ultimate form of sovereignty.

8. Crowgito Ergo Sum

Call it a crisis, but Crow reached a point where he felt that a total reassessment was necessary—a full-on epistemological inventory. He looked in the mirror, metaphorically speaking, and didn't have much feeling for what he saw. After all this time, and so many minor victories in a hoarded life, what had he actually accomplished? Bottom line, not much. Nothing like what the legends, myths, and old wives' tales would lead one to expect. No feats of divination or quasi-divine transformation (Don J notwithstanding, Crow was still a bird), not even any overt acts of rebellion or grand theft. There were various children he had left behind, somewhere, but they weren't in touch with him. Friends, lovers—he'd had them, and it wasn't like they came around much, either. Why should they? Crow was, probably, recriminating too much, given the generally low expectations of the biome. No bird or other creature ever demanded much of anything from him. Still, why so little in the bank—again, metaphorically speaking?

Perhaps because everything Crow knew was wrong. Not delusional, not egotistical, just flat out wrong. It meant his actions, down to the smallest gesture, were taken in a mist of error and speculation.

The dilemma came on him in a moment of indefinable anxiety. Crow was watching a caterpillar—not a type he found edible—inch its way up the trunk of a tree, when he reflected, first, that there was absolutely nothing in the outward form of the thing that logically suggested what it would become. In other words, from one stage to the next no necessary connection seemed to exist. It was preposterous, but he had seen it happen, seen the cocoons festooning trees and seen the winged versions emerge later, but just because it had happened was no guarantee it would happen ever again. Anomalous events seemed to be occurring everywhere. Or something else might happen. It might, for example, become Imelda Marcos's shoe collection, or something never seen before, a new planet the color of jade. So, thus, likewise, in the second place, his own existence was not guaranteed from one instant to the next, and not just because some load of toxic sludge might suddenly fall from the sky. No. There was simply no certainty that one day, one moment, one instant would lead to the next, with him present in it. Everything was unprecedented, a cosmic one-off. What if the past, as he sensed it, was simply an instantaneous creation repeated? He was nothing but a collection of discontinuous instants. Ditto the universe. It wasn't a question of belief. You could believe in anything, tell yourself any story you want. It wasn't the same as knowing.

No wonder he couldn't get anything done. Perhaps this was all fallout from Crow's encounter with that Yucatan jay, but he suspected he would have come to this cul-de-sac anyway.

What did he really know? Of what could he be sure? Very possibly the entire notion of a *he,* or rather an *I,* was the biggest illusion of all, the ultimate in hypostasizing. But how could he go forward without some foundation of, if not certainty, at least a philosophy of "as if"? While the caterpillar made its way toward transformation, Crow decided to take stock. And unlike some radical nihilist, he would not posit an evil demiurge who fabricated everything in order to deceive him. He would not take the void as his purpose just to avoid purposelessness. He would not doubt his experience. He would examine it in order to discover what he might trust, if only to build a sense of possibility. Trust, that was it. If he could trust anything about the world, he might be able to trust himself to take the next step. This is what he thought he knew:

1. What goes up must come down.

2. To prevent the high pick and roll, blitz the point guard.

3. You can't step in the same river.

4. The early bird catches the worm, if and only if the worm itself is also early.

5. Big fish eat little fish.

6. Little fish eat littler fish.

7. Those fish eat something else, so everything ultimately depends on "something else."

8. If it seems like the worst, it isn't.

9. The sun rises, having no apparent choice, on the nothing new.

10. Zen is nothing.

11. No progress without contraries, but as yet no progress is detectable.

12. There is no natural religion.

13. To generalize is to be an idiot.

14. Bald eagles are not bald.

15. Dumbbells are not dumb, nor are they bells.

16. Never wager your head or any other body part in a bet you think you can't lose.

17. Absence of pleasure in the animal kingdom is a semantic problem. Among plants, no speculation is possible.

18. Pain hurts.

19. You can't hide from those who don't want to find you.

20. Many cannot come from one, and yet they do.

21. Nevertheless, we find a great deal to say about what cannot be said.

22. No peacock ever hid its tail.

23. Snakes are ominous because they have no necks.

24. If you forgot it once, you'll forget it again.

25. The fucking you get isn't worth the fucking you take.

This last came from Crow's father, a bit of received wisdom if ever there was such. Nevertheless, Crow found it almost without exception to be true.

These fragments Crow, the maker of lists, shored up against his ruin.

9. Crow Vagabond

Somehow Crow must have missed the announcement, or was it a neutron bomb or *les vacances* at the wrong time of year, or an obscure holiday or a workers' strike that emptied Paris? Of all the cities in the world, Paris was the one city for dreaming in, even for the natives who were stuck here and thought life would be hipper, faster, cheaper in New York. (Crow the anglo was not there to disabuse anyone of their illusions.) But it was vacant! *Vide!* What had happened?

It had never been the old myths that drew Crow, oysters and champagne at La Coupole. What drew him were the places to roost, the places from which to see and be seen. At every corner, on every street, there were pediments, towers, spires, sills, and balustrades. Balconies. Cornices. Wedding-cake vestiges of the Baroque. *Aux anciens parapets!* True, there were pigeons to contend with, and they acted like they owned the place, their disdain evident (envy likewise). But many of them came from places like Angoulême, Besançon, and Roubaix, and now they seemed to have gone back where they came from, revealing their true provincial selves and taking their accents with them. *Vide!*

The lights were coming on, the city was jeweled for the evening about to begin. How sweet it was to watch the night open its eyes in this city! But there was no one on the sidewalks, and even in the few passing cars, Crow could barely detect the drivers. It was almost as if they were hunkered down so low the cars were driving themselves. A city in amber, thought Crow, a relic unearthed by some cataclysmic event, or frozen by it. *Personne.* Crow made a pass by the *pétanque* ground in the Luxembourg gardens, but the players had all vanished. Where was the teen-age punk rocker with the torn T-shirt who carried her balls in a vintage Pan Am flight bag and pitched so perfectly she made the pot-bellied old men laugh, although they tried not to show it? They hung up their sport coats so carefully on the clothing racks they had set up. Not like the players at the funky ground near Stalingrad and the canal, who never laughed at all, deadly serious. Crow could have watched for hours.

Trash was beginning to pile up along the streets, like dust breeding. The Promenade Plantée looked like a potters' field, a ragged natural revenge. How arid it was! How fertile it was! A battleground from which the decimated armies had departed, leaving the spoils to Crow. The city was his; he was the last *flâneur*, on, above, and along the boulevards, the only one left to testify to the pleasures of the street. But what pleasures now? Without the passing display, Crow felt his isolation, his existential quiddity. Let the philosophers insist that hell is others. In this city, those others were his show of shows. His beak clacked dissatisfaction with the freedom of solitude, and the sound came back to him like the dull "*pétanque*" of metal on metal.

Crow needed cheering up in the very place that had never let him down, even in the worst weather, in ice storms and cataclysmic wind events and the Sahel that somehow managed to make it this far north every summer, boiling the elderly in their garrets. He marshalled the strength to make a trip out to the *Jardin d'Acclimitation*, but when he got to the *jardin*, the gates were closed, *les attractions* silent. He pecked disconsolately at a discarded packet of *frites*.

Crow endured a very difficult night in the City of Light. From

Montmartre to the Place d'Italie, from the Champs de Mars out to La Défense, lights glittered like a jeweled wrist snapping a gesture of dismissal, and Crow understood the loneliness of the outsider, the global tourist become vagabond, bereft of fantasy and projection. The Seine cut a dark rift through it all, like Crow's mood. How many birds had deliberately plunged into that darkness?

That night, Crow perched on the agonized iron sculptures of the Pont de Bir-Hakeim. How could he forget, how could he not fail to remember, his first view of the city? He had felt gauche, naïve, ingenuous, as if a great secret had been hidden from him all along, a secret everyone knew but him, even though he had been almost everywhere. It was the secret of how to live. But just now, returning after so long, when he felt he knew more than enough and the city would reward him as it does every jaded soul with the wonder of rejuvenation, Crow found he was too late. The city was locked down, under a pandemic siege, and he had had enough. When the sun came up, Crow made a final pass over the Louvre and the Tuileries just as the mist in the park was beginning to burn off. He thought, without the shadows, light could not ride these magnificent objects. The sun would have to go on foot, like a beggar. That was when he saw her.

She was a squat and solid older woman, with a page boy haircut, an N95 mask, sensible shoes, a long black skirt, and a bright-colored heavy sweater, even though it was late spring. What got Crow's attention, however, was the apparatus she stood next to and was fiddling with, a three-legged scarecrow with a box on top. She adjusted the thing, pulled up a black cloth that hung from the back of the box, then put her head under the cloth for an instant. When she emerged with a cord in hand, she took one last look and squeezed a bulb on the end of a cord. Then she flipped up the cloth, pulled a square frame from the back of the machine, and slipped it into a case sitting on the ground. Her actions were meticulous and routine. Crow liked the mechanical precision of routines. He stopped to watch.

By now, the sun was up, and the mist was gone, replaced by a clear view of the evenly planted parallel rows of elm trees along the *grande allée*. The woman studied them for a minute, picked up the case, and in a single strong motion snapped up the stand with its box and walked with a purpose to a spot much farther on, in front of a sculpture of a lion with a peacock in its mouth. (Skeptical of the hubris of peacocks, Crow was nevertheless deeply ambivalent about the theme.) She regarded it warily, almost as if it were alive, then stepped back a safe distance, set up, repeated her entire operation. She proceeded to do the same thing for many of the sculptures in the vast park, including another spectacular one of a lion trashing a crocodile. (Crow approved of the theme.) Crow was so used to seeing people with their phones and strap-supported cameras everywhere he flew that it took him all this time to realize the woman was photographing. By the time he figured it out, she had packed up her camera, tripod, and case in the same matter-of-fact way, walked to her car (an antique Citroën, illegally parked, but there weren't any other cars around), and put the gear in the front passenger seat.

Crow watched her take off like a bat out of hell. Well, that was cheering. A Parisian eccentric with a lead foot, probably an animal advocate, although on a domestic level those types tended to favor cats. But good to see they were still operating in the face of whatever had banished the rest of humanity and most of the avian life from the city. Crow pondered. If hell is others, *les autres*, presumably that is because they observe you, define you, and otherwise limit who you might be. On the other hand, you also looked at them, and, whether or not you made any claim on their so-called freedom, you would be observing, and thereby expanding your *self*, your being, the amplitude of your consciousness. Hell is others, but it is also sort of heaven. *Pas de banalités*, Crow. Crow lifted off looking for the Citroën.

The longer Crow followed her, the less he was able to separate his love of the places she visited from the woman herself, attentive, patient, assiduous, crazy. She looked into doorways and stairways, store windows with manikins not yet dressed. Traveling with her, Crow saw a starfish drawn on an ancient shoe last, like a foot that had scraped the ocean floor. The bookshops with their fussy window displays hinted at the chaos of human knowledge and dying worlds within. The books on offer, held open by rubber bands, proclaimed themselves in a riot of typefaces. If you stopped to look, you were already ossified, too. She stopped in front of each one, to consider it as a candidate for her archive.

Following her, Crow felt once again how the narrow streets so often ended in the sight of some monument—Les Invalides or the Panthéon or Saint-Sulpice. And if a bird were to turn his back on those and plunge more deeply into the labyrinth, he would find himself deposited out of the dark winding channel into the calm pool of an empty *place*, the Square of the Innocents or the Place Monge, there to reclaim his bearings. You could always gain altitude, if that was so important to know where you were, but after all, what difference did it make to be lost in such a city?

She was indefatigable, renewed each morning by the light across the city and concluding only when the light began to fade. She seemed to know every back street in Paris, every trick around Montmartre and Belleville, or maybe it was the Citroën that knew, or the camera. Crow never fully accepted the idea that *les voitures* were nonliving beings. He had seen too much unpredictable behavior on the roadways to believe that.

Crow questioned how long she (and by extension he) might go on. He also wondered what the photographs actually looked like. But at least he was seeing what she saw, and so he was himself a kind of camera. If only memory were as indelible as those images on film. Crow was already beginning to forget where they had been. But she would always know, always have the pictures.

When she walked out of the Place des Vosges and headed down the rue des Rosiers, Crow barely had the energy to follow. And when the old woman came to a corner café, one of the few still unshuttered and advertising glatt kosher, and plunked herself down at a streetside table, Crow didn't care whether she shooed him away. He landed on the chair across from her. No sense pretending at this point that he wasn't following her.

She had leaned her camera and tripod against the door frame of the café, and the masked waiter, who seemed like he was half asleep since there was not a single other customer on the entire street, had to navigate around the beast to get to the table. He already carried a steaming demitasse and a small plate with a single rugelach. *Voilà, madame Agnès, comme d'habitude.* Another routine, it seemed. She sipped the espresso, took a small bite of the rugelach, and pushed the plate in Crow's direction. Crow was in no mood to refuse. This was his moveable feast.

They looked each other over against the backdrop of the clean, well-lighted place.

The woman looked at Crow. "In another life, you might be one of us. You certainly have the patience for it. We've been doing this for a long time."

But not the obsession. He could not quite understand why she did what she did, and why so many others, who looked a bit like ghosts, now that he thought of it, did the same.

She took another sip of esprsso and poured another drop on Crow's plate. Then she said, "Because this machine never talks back to me, and it knows the secrets of the city. When it was invented, it created an army of people like me. Charles, Eugène, Andre, Henri, Lisette, Robert, Germaine, Willy, Ilsa. If we did not do this, everything you see would cease to exist. It would be like waking up from a dream and finding yourself in an empty room. The present time has taught what emptiness feels like." She finished the coffee. Then she added, "I'd like to know what you see. Does this café look empty to you? Does the street? Perhaps it's because the people I've watched come here year after year, always in the same places, are so familiar they have become phantoms. I scarcely notice them, but my camera registers them. It's more likely that it is me who is becoming a ghost."

With that she stood up and set some coins on the saucer. The waiter arrived at the sound, picked up the plate, and shook them into his apron. She took the tripod and set it up a few steps into the street. She pointed the lens at Crow. At this point, Crow couldn't have flown away if he had wanted to. The round aperture seemed less like an eye and more like a well that might swallow him.

"Now, Crow, you have a twin," she said. "There will always be another you."

Yet which now came first, the bird or its double? The picture or the place? Which would come last? he wondered. In a thousand years, when everything was gone and Paris itself was crumpled up and tossed away, there might still be a crow who would somehow see this picture, with the empty cup and the bored waiter, and intuit all the mythologies of the past, of plagues and longing transformed into a thin and vivid oracle. Not Crow in particular but his place in all this. Crow imagined his own passing and was strangely consoled. Wasn't that what pictures were really for? Wasn't that what the city was for anyway? A place not to remember and mourn particular losses but a place to imagine, a place not to confirm any fact but simply to provide a pretext, a profound occasion to invent. *L'invitation au voyage.*

10. Crow Married
(for R.S.K.)

Crow had a reputation as a serial monogamist, but with a remarkable capacity to empathize with his past liaisons—partners, hook-ups, what to call them? Truth be told, he didn't see them much, and more than once they didn't recognize him. That was kind of a bummer. He remembered a Hawaiian honeycreeper (really!) had once said to him, "I'd like to remember you just as you are, so in order to do that, you'll have to leave now." She was a redhead, and even though her wings smelled like an old tent, he had trouble letting go.

His relationships followed the line of least resistance, until they resisted. He never looked too far ahead or planned for a future he didn't believe in. Be in the moment, he reminded himself. When Crow was in a relationship (however), he liked to talk, and it had led to some interesting conversations. Like the time he and his steady were sitting on a fence looking at a scarecrow for entertainment (limited) while a farmer planted his field. Crow was engaged in a disquisition about how corn was a new-world crop and the Mayans had coined the word for it, when she said to him, "Crow, you're a McCormick manure spreader with a vocabulary attachment." She was the same one who said to Crow after an argument about how self-centered he was, "I don't think you've said much of anything, but I feel better." That was one of the nicer things she said, and she seemed actually to like him.

The San Quentin quail he chalked up to youthful indiscretion. Neither of them had any idea that state-line statutes applied to the animal kingdom. And besides, nobody transported anybody; they were both on their own wing. She needed a break from her family.

The one that really got in his head was the Stellar's jay. Crow had a thing for jays. He liked that they were super aggressive, and even though they could clean up, there was something trashy and overdone about them. Just like him, they weren't afraid to make noise. Sheila looked a little unbalanced, like she might be on something, but she made Crow right away. "You fuck with me and I'll peck your eyes out. Just remember the littlest hen can take on the biggest cock." Was that supposed to be sexual? As with so many things that might have seemed obvious, Crow wasn't sure.

He sometimes kidded her that she reminded him of a cocktail waitress in a Dolly Parton wig. They had a lot of fun.

One day she said to him, "You know your problem, Crow, is that you don't know how to manage expectations." What on earth did that mean? Whose expectations? Hers or his? Expectations for what? Was that a way of saying he was an incurable romantic? Nothing lasts forever, cool. No illusions there. Or did she mean manage *her* desires, her demands, her wishes, her beliefs, fantasies, regrets, visions of the present and future? Crow suddenly felt the true burden of the Other, whose center is forever elsewhere, not one with yours.

In retrospect, the breakup was probably inevitable, and it wasn't the offspring thing. Yes, there was a species issue, but Crow was pretty sure there must be a way around that, given the state of biomedical science. It went down differently, an embarrassing melodrama. One day Crow circled by her nest unexpectedly (for her). From a distance, he could see the familiar colors, the flash of blue, black and white. Except they weren't hers. Another jay, an American blue jay, totally middle class, with all the acquisitive energy of the thoughtless go getter. Whom, he was sure, she would refer to as a good provider. Crow was not a very good provider, although he had plans. So that was that. He didn't stop by to pick up his stuff.

Crow sang the blues. In spite of his terrible voice, he felt he'd earned it:

Black crow in the cornfield,
Looks like he been sleepin' all day.
He been flyin' so high,
Looks like he done lost his way.

A friend of his—everybody called the bird Crow-magnon—pulled Crow aside and gave him some unsolicited advice. "It really is a species problem," he said. "I hate to sound like some kind of nationalist or luddite, but you need to stick to your own kind. You just found out that blood is thicker than water." Is that what he learned? Or did he discover, yet again, that love wasn't all it was cracked up to be? After that, Crow went on a weird jag. It's not that he swore off pleasures, more that he realized he had overlooked something important. How to put this politely: He haunted other birds' nests. Wherever he heard the sound of chicks, he would roost nearby, watching the atavistic open-mouthed featherless bundles and the precise feeding. The mothers seemed to strike with such force that they couldn't possibly avoid hurting the babies, and yet they never did. The beaks never went too far; the small heads always pulled back just enough to take nourishment. They exchanged a knowledge beyond communicating.

There were mothers and fathers who were sacrificially fierce in defense of their young. What did they know?

Unfortunately, on a couple of occasions this innocent observational habit drew attention that jerked Crow out of his reverie. In the fall, he was assailed by a flock of migrating sandhill cranes, thousands of them, who pursued him through the treetops of Mendocino County. They were big and were likely to roll all over him. Crow wasn't fast, but he had endurance and adrenaline, and he outlasted them, beating along until he could no longer hear the cries of "Pervert!" "Peeping Tom!" "Sicko!" He wanted to tell them how beautiful they were and how the new life they pursued so heedlessly had the capacity to save the world.

Crow found it mesmerizing, in spite of a certain lack of variety in the domestic situations, regardless of species. Crow could barely watch the moments of first flight, cruel but fair. Was there not another endpoint, a more durable purpose beyond the swift horizontal business he had known? A pleasure beyond pleasure. How could he never have noticed something so basic? Crow thought: If I can remember what I was at the very beginning, before all this disappointment, when someone like me knew unconditional love, then I can love and be faithful.

The singularity he had once cultivated now felt like a chronic illness, threatening to turn into something much worse. He had never looked outside himself for help, and now when he did there was none. But at least, at last, he knew what he wanted: someone who could frame things with a different set of concepts, more precise than the ones he used. Someone whose moves could mimic sunlight and whose sounds describe moonlight wakefulness. *Thou wast not born for death, immortal bird.* Those kinds of sounds. Someone the same but completely different, a symbol and a cipher, transparent and opaque, through which the world can be seen, beyond which it cannot be imagined.

One thing for sure, he would know the answer when he saw it on the wing and heard its song. He would know what he could trust. Until then, he would practice patience and, when necessary, sacrifice.

11. Crow's Trip

Someone left the cake out in the rain. It could have been all the sweet green icing flowing down that got Crow's attention. It certainly wasn't any sentiment about how long it must have taken to bake it, or the sense that he would never have that recipe again. He knew that what is sweet now turns so sour. He had no teeth, but if he had, he would have had to have them all pulled out after a taste of this Savoy truffle, this cream tangerine, or whatever it was. He was no gourmand. He liked to pick.

The whole gooey thing made Crow flash back to when he was eight miles high, how everything around him looked like a strange gray town, known for its sounds, with sidewalk scenes and black limousines, shapeless forms, some just hanging around. Nowhere was there warmth to be found among those afraid of losing their ground. Eight miles high? Eight miles out of Memphis, more like, and he had no friends, eight miles straight up downtown somewhere. He felt he needed something, a mother's little helper or a pill to make him larger, or one to make him small. But the one that mother gave him didn't do anything at all. There was always Mister Jimmy, but man, did he look pretty ill. Crow would certainly never trust some hookah-smoking character, or a gypsy with a gold tattoo and a pad on 34th and Vine, even less a bunch of pigeons on a chessboard sidewalk standing up and telling him where to go. But he had to do something because he'd just had some kind of mushroom and his mind was moving on. He needed to feed his head, not his body. He figured he would go ask Alice, as long as the red queen hadn't totally lost her head. On the other hand, he could ask the Mississippi Queen, the Cajun, down around Vicksburg, but she'd already taught him everything.

Best to check with Alice. You could get anything you wanted at her restaurant, even if you were feathered. Hot rats? Hot zits? Peaches en regalia? The odd thing was, she never served anything green. Why was a vegetable always something to hide? If you called on any vegetable, called it by name, a rutabaga, for instance, Crow was pretty sure the vegetable would respond to you. He suddenly felt like crying 96 tears. They were tears of rage, tears of grief. Why, he wondered, was he always destined to be the thief? He was more like a wicked messenger, with a mind that multiplied the smallest matter. But he was a free bird, was he not? He could walk down the street and there was no one there, though the pavement was one huge crowd. He could fly down the road his eyes didn't see, though his mind wanted to cry out loud. He had been waiting so long to be where he was going—in the sunshine of someone's love.

He'd take the world in a love embrace because the long and short of it was that he was a true Nature's child, he was born to be wild. He liked smoke and lightning, heavy-metal thunder. Racing with the wind and the feeling he was under. Yeah, he'd make it happen, but first Crow would just drop in to see what condition his condition was in. He pushed his soul into a deep dark hole, and then he followed it in. He watched himself crawling out as he was crawling in. Across Itchykoo Park, or maybe it was MacArthur Park, over by the zoo. Someone, he couldn't remember who, had told him it was all happening at the zoo, with its insincere giraffes and skeptical orangutans. Even the hamsters turned on frequently. He thought he heard those damned pigeons again, plotting in secrecy. But as he drew closer, he realized the pigeons were philosophizing. One was clinking a tiny set of cymbals and nodding rhythmically. The other had shaved her head. They were talking about the space between us all and the creatures who hide themselves behind the wall of illusion. They don't know, he heard them whisper. They can't see, until it's much too late. They were talking about the love that's grown so cold and the creatures who gain the world but lose their soul. Crow asked himself: Are they talking about me? Am I one of *them*? Meanwhile, life flowed on within him and without him.

Crow sensed himself touching down, and he was finding that things were stranger than he had ever known. When you're strange, he thought, faces come out of the rain. When you're strange, no one remembers your name. If only he could remember his own name. He just couldn't get any satisfaction. That was the issue; it was always the issue, always had been the issue. He thought the leaden winter would bring him down forever. There was nothing in his little red book that could ever replace the charm of good vibrations, but how to get them happening again? He imagined riding a crimson shell, like Aphrodite, to the violence of the sun. He imagined tiny purple fishes, laughing. Maybe, on the other hand, he should just leave on a jet plane—to save his wings—and not care when he'd be back again. There had been so many times he'd played around, so many times he'd let everyone down. Better to come back maybe next week, after he was off this losing streak?

Crow saw a red door and wanted it painted black, that's how bummed he felt, like he was in a white room with black curtains near a station, where the shadows ran from themselves. He looked inside himself and saw his heart was black. He wanted to see the sun blotted out from the sky. He was going down. His crow's feet were out the window, and his head was on the ground. No sun coming through that window, like he was living at the bottom of a grave. It's true. He didn't live today. Maybe tomorrow, he just couldn't say. He used to laugh about everybody that was hanging out. Now he wasn't laughing so loud. Now he wasn't feeling so proud. Especially about having to scrounge up his next meal. He caught a glimpse of himself in a street window. He looked like a penguin. No way. More like a surfing bird. But a bird after all was just a word. Crow would have to believe in magic to get beyond that. How the music could free him whenever it starts. That it was his special friend and it intended him to dance on fire. But the music was over, and maybe it was time to turn out the lights. Kicks were getting harder to find, and his kicks weren't bringing him peace of mind. It was a hard world to get a break in because all the good things had been taken. Briefly, very briefly, he was confident enough to think that maybe there was a way to make certain things pay, and though he was dressed in rags, he'd wear silk one day. They could treat him unkind, but someday he'd treat them refined. He could still recall the times he cried, but he'd break on through to the other side.

Some day. Some way. Even though the day destroys the night, and the night divides the day. But for now, he knew how it felt to be on his own, a complete unknown. No one, he concluded, was in his tree, though it must be high or low. That is, he couldn't, you know, tune in, but it was all right, that is, he thought maybe it wasn't too bad. But when the rain comes, he'd for sure have to run and hide his head. He might as well be dead. On the other hand, deep down he knew that whether it rains or shines, it's just a state of mind. Crow tried to hold that thought, but time kept on slipping, slipping into the future.

In a purple haze, Crow found himself standing next to a mountain. He chopped it down with the edge of his wing. He picked up all the pieces and made an island. He even raised a little sand. He was sure he didn't figure anymore in this world, but maybe he would meet someone in the next one, and he wouldn't be late. Crow looked down from his lonely wooden tower—he preferred to think of it that way and not as a badly constructed scarecrow. He knew that only drowning creatures could see him. See me! Feel me! he wanted to caw at them. Touch me! Heal me! And while you're at it, if I swallow anything evil, stick your beak down my throat. But all he heard in response was the sound of silence, nothing more than the words of empty prophets, written on subway walls. And tenement halls. (Crow had never actually been inside a tenement, although alleyways, for sure.)

He'd had too much to dream last night, that was it. Too much to dream. He couldn't bear the visions racing through his head. It was all so real he could still feel his own eagerness, but when his wings reached out for something to caress . . . came the dawn, and it was gone, gone, gone.

No, not yet. It was getting *near* dawn, when lights close their tired eyes. All the while he was, taking his time, lying there staring at the ceiling, waiting for that sleepy feeling. It never came. He wasn't ready to face the light. Maybe he never would be.

But everybody seemed to think he was lazy. He didn't mind. He thought they were crazy, running everywhere at such a speed. Eventually they would find there was no need. He was truckin. He had his chips cashed in. It had, after all, been a long, strange trip. No wonder everybody he knew said he was changed. Laughing behind their wings, they said he was strange.

But he knew all he needed was love, love is all you need. There was nothing he could know that wasn't known. Nothing he could show that wasn't shown. Nowhere he could be that wasn't where he was meant to be. It was easy. Things were clearer than before, showing him the way, asking him to stay. He'd never close the door on all these things and more, in his mind's eye.

He'd never close the door in his mind's eye.

12. Ice Cream for Crow

(for G. Crawford)

Los Angeles was a bitch. Crow found himself rehearsing the top ten reasons why long-term habitation was out of the question:

1. Fire

2. Fire

3. Smoke and the inevitability of COPD

4. Lack of rainfall (and the concomitant likelihood of fire)

5. The Disney Concert Hall (once singed, twice shy)

6. The disappearance of orange groves

7. Conversational deficits of a one-company town. ("Crow, did you hear about the credits for the new Coen brothers' film? 'Avian assistants.' They're *named*, and they get serious screen time.") Crow made a pact with himself to avoid premiers, especially in West Hollywood.

8. A pervasive mix of condescension and insecurity

9. A pervasive mix of generalized ambition and personal indifference

10. The In-N-Out Burger. Crow learned by hard experience that a strong pair of wings will get you into the drive-through lane, but it won't get you out.

As soon as he arrived, the first thing anyone said to him was, "So when are you moving to LA?" As if his mere presence constituted some sort of buy-in, a definitive affirmation. Luckily Crow didn't drive a car, could live in Brentwood if he wanted, and liked midcentury-modern architecture and even the dumpster-diving eclecticism of Beverly Hills. Needless to say, he didn't have to depend on the nonexistent public transportation system.

Fires notwithstanding, it should have worked out. Maybe the main problem was that Crow was not a beach creature and didn't need even the idea of it. After only a few hours at Malibu, watching the surfers repeat themselves, ditto the shorebirds, wheeling and diving, Crow began to develop a theory. It had to do with the momentum of an eternal day and the terminal coast. In the East, the sun rose, you never knew exactly from where since you never actually saw it rise. It was dark, and then it was light, and you went about your business. Given where the beaches lay, sunset was usually interrupted by at least four mountain ranges and twenty states. If you wanted more and were desperate for every last minute, you had to look west. It was not exactly the land of never-ending promise, but no wonder the beaches out here were always crowded. Back East it was already dark. That momentum would carry you right to shore and even beyond.

Crow never experienced the dread of the East and its opposite desire. Instead, he felt that he would rather be living in Siberia than go through another parking lot day in the City of Angels, heavy with smog and libidinal frustration. Everybody said it would be way easier to get laid in LA, way. But it still didn't rain, and sure enough, there was Crow in another parking lot, this one in a mini mall, in front of Beverly Soon's Tofu Restaurant. It was not entirely by accident. Crow had to admit that the possibilities of ethnic cuisine were exceptional in LA, and if you were the sort to accept what was on offer, then it was best to put yourself in a position where what was on offer was likely to be at least interesting. Crow never met pickier eaters than in this town. He kept hearing complaints about there being no good Burmese food in Silver Lake.

Beverly Soon's was not much to look at, tucked in among an acupuncture studio, a computer repair shop, and a travel agency. Crow had heard how the kitchen staff was preindustrial in their relation to birds, always kept track of who liked what and how much to leave out front, but the birds had to do their part. Keep a lid on it, too big a crowd and they would all be rousted. It worked fine, and Crow came specifically to see if, in a town based on hype, this place would live up to it.

He never found out. It was, as usual, blistering hot when he landed in the parking lot. He saw in front of him a vast pool of glistening water. (Crow loved the swimming pools of LA, the favorite feature of his flyovers, and he was worried that some water-control edict would shut them down. That would be like beautiful lapis lazuli beads being lopped off a necklace, one at a time.) Crow was parched. The lake seemed to be a mirage of water. But it wasn't—either a mirage or water. He failed to notice that the balcony above Beverly Soon's housed a liquor store and that the "lake" issued from several smashed cartons of mezcal bottles obviously dropped off the balcony during delivery. Crow needed relief before he could think straight, much less about kimchee. He drank, and drank some more, despite the odd taste. It tasted like tarmac. Well, what did you expect? Before he knew it, he was staggering, and before he knew *that*, he was already on his back. Too late for prophylactic Advil! Crow was blitzed, trashed, snockered, pie-eyed, blotto, wasted, looped, stewed, pickled. Out cold, while the rest of the world ran away like horses over the hills.

When he woke up the sun was going down. He was as desiccated as an old sponge. He could hear someone opening a refuse bin nearby. Anything but that: West Coast trash, skid row, more disposable than the latest miniseries, like some character from a Bukowski novel. Just at that moment, a Toyota Forerunner rolled up, the door opened, and out stepped a woman in a muumuu, a bushy bun hairdo, moth tattoos everywhere, and flip-flops. She had a towel in her hand. She studied Crow. Crow studied her, crookedly. "It looks alive, Grey. Let's work a little benevolence. It will be a good karmic thing." With that she wrapped Crow up.

When he came to again, he had to deal with his first hangover, and the fact that he was in a wicker cage, something for a parrot, he figured. But there was fruit juice—or maybe it was the remnants of a smoothie—in a dish and some kelp puff snacks. The cage was hanging outside the kitchen above the patio. He tried to figure out where he was, based on the view into the backyard and his extensive knowledge of the domestic LA topography. It looked like a bungalow near La Brea. Thank God. Anything but Venice. The kelp puffs weren't bad as a salt-delivery system.

"You're up. And you're eating. That's good." The woman was now dressed in spandex workout clothes. She carried a bottle of ichorous green stuff that she occasionally sucked through a straw. It interested Crow strangely. She was joined by her friend? Husband? Partner? Roommate? Crow knew things were fluid these days. He was tall with a silver ponytail. He looked like someone you would see on a poster for a B+ movie about survivalists in Idaho.

Grey looked closely at Crow. "What do we call him? Crows are smart. They respond to names."

"How do you know he's not a she? And besides, maybe it self-identifies differently."

"Ah. My bad. But 'it' is so objectifying. We'll keep it generic and just say Crow, no pronouns." Then he added, "Sorry about the cage. You gotta get right, bird. It's a jungle out there."

So began a kind of routine: food followed by conversation and then activities. Over the space of two days this included the deposit of various interesting objects in the cage: poker chips in three colors, several beaded necklaces, some bottle caps. Best of all was a tiny puzzle of some sunflowers in bilious yellow. Crow had never seen a puzzle before, but when they stood the box up against the cage and Crow could see the picture, he began to get the idea. It took him awhile to assemble the pieces, not because he didn't know how they set up but because he couldn't get them to stick together. Fragments, but their order was crystal clear.

"Grey, looks like we have the cubist Van Gogh."

"Very cool. Wonder what he—sorry—Crow would do with mahjong tokens or dominoes."

By the next day, Crow was out of the cage and on the kitchen table. He and Grey instantly became domino opponents. The game was rule based and almost too easy. Sometimes Crow was rewarded with a tidbit. He especially liked pad Thai. He paid attention and figured out that the treat was a consequence and definition of winning. Hence, also the reason to play. He was slightly obsessed and would battle Grey until the man's eyes glazed over. After that, for much of the day, with his air space restricted, things were pretty boring.

Which was when the crows arrived. Crow heard them before he saw them, at least two dozen nested in a large fig tree. A voice said, "Brother, good to see you back in business and keeping in shape during your incarceration."

Crow thought, Where were you when I needed you? But he was touched that they had bothered to pay a visit. "To what do I owe the honor?" he cawed.

"Honor? No honor, brother, just a solid. We saw you in a bad state—no judgments about that—and then renditioned. We look out for each other. Maybe that's unfamiliar to you, what with the East Coast thing of everyone for himself, every tub on its own bottom, get your claws off my stack. We tend to be bigger picture out here, a sense of the whole, connectedness, if you know what I mean."

"Appreciate the thought, and I'm not gonna lie, I have learned some things from watching you, like that trick about dropping the walnuts on Pico so the cars will crush them. But what did you mean about incarceration? And 'rendition'?"

"So maybe you haven't recovered enough to notice the apparatus that surrounds you. If I ask you to join us out here, what happens?"

Crow hadn't actually paid much attention to his accommodations except to notice that the service was getting better and better. But he didn't have to play with the door to know he couldn't get the cage open.

"Listen, don't worry about me. I've got a plan. I'm gonna play my way out of this. But I'm not quite ready to split. I think I sprained my neck. I wouldn't last two seconds back in the world. Just let me know where y'all hang out, and I'll be in touch."

There was a general clucking from the tree, the sound of pitying condescension. "Okay. Cool. We can tell by your tone of voice that this go-it-alone individual consciousness thing is hard to give up. But prison can be place of investigation and clarity. It has helped a lot of birds see the light. You'll find that the apparent benevolence of your captors is simply that: a façade." Before Crow could answer, a cry went up: "Free Crow! Free Crow! Free Crow!"

Crow measured again the confines of his cage. What was the nature of freedom, after all?

"Grey, this is wild. Are you listening to these crows? They are going nuts. What are they talking about, do you think?"

"They could be talking about us. And what they are saying probably isn't very nice. It's hard to argue with a cage. Anyway, I brought some ice cream for Crow, a new flavor, 'Nine Miles of Bad Road.' It's got all kinds of chunky stuff in it for him—sorry, for *Crow*—to play with."

Crow spent the rest of the day picking apart the stuff in the dish after he had consumed the ice cream part. As much as he knew about human civilization, this seemed to be the apex of it. There was ginger, chocolate, various dried fruits, a wide range of nuts, kelp (again!), amaranth, and freekeh. Mad eclecticism! Such an arrangement of incompatible elements! Either this was an organized chaos of sensations—his initial impression of LA in toto—or it was an invitation to contemplate another order of experience. Was this something his friends in the tree already understood or something, perhaps, that in their racial paranoia they had never known, never even suspected? They were keeping unnervingly silent. There was an occasional murmur of, "Well, you could share. That would be a good first step."

The next morning, after a sleepless night of self-scrutiny, Crow watched his "captors" set up a table for breakfast on the patio, pour a smoothie into a dish, and open the cage. Crow stepped out onto the table. It was as if the world were new. The jacaranda and bougainvillea almost put him into a swoon. This, too, was LA. He hopped over and took a hit of the smoothie. Grey was looking at him intently. "The cage is open, Crow, and I'm not going to close it. You don't need it anymore."

Crow looked up into the tree. All the crows were still there. He could not forget about them. They wouldn't let him. "Remember how sweet those walnuts were? Sweeter than any gift you might be given here. You are barely a bird here, Crow. A companion animal, a mere pet. Remember that."

Barely a bird, yes, but a bird in a great house. Crow stood at the edge of the cage.

"What's it going to be," said one of crows after a while.

What's it going to be? thought Crow.

13. Crow Kneels in Protest

Crow had never participated in organized sports and never trusted the animals, including and especially people, who did. He liked to think of himself as a practitioner of autonomous fitness, and he didn't need to do much to stay in shape. He was, after all, born that way, and the only morbidly obese birds he ever saw—leaving aside what he knew about chickens and penguins, of course, who needed the insulation—were otherwise incarcerated. Better call a spade a spade than use euphemisms, like "circus performers," "pets," "companion animals," and "therapy birds." (He knew firsthand it was pretty good on the inside of a cage, and the fact of overweight canaries lent some cred to that.) Not that he couldn't appreciate coordinated effort and collective activities. Watching geese form a perfect V as they migrated and then keep it together as long as they were in flight, no matter what, was maybe the most impressive thing Crow had ever seen. And the red knots that migrate from the top of the globe to the bottom, from the Arctic to the southern tip of South America, nothing he knew of could compare with that. He watched the birds scatter and re-form without commands or hesitation, a kind of deep group-think Crow almost envied. It never changed, and he never got tired of it, season after season.

But it seemed there always had to be someone in charge, someone calling the shots, someone at the apex of the wedge, the captain, the "motivator," the "mentor." Crow hated coaches, authority figures of any kind for that matter, with their whistles, charts, and narrow evaluation systems. They were all cut from the same cloth, the kind that would push you off the edge of the nest and yell, "Fly!" like that was some sort of instruction, some sort of life lesson. Crow was no mere instrument, no position player, driven to a berserk edge by mindless repetition and the demonization of opponents. Crow was Crow, the best available athlete, many tooled. He would fly over a soccer field and feel like cawing, "I'm a free agent. Talk to my people. You can't afford me." You want me to stand for the so-called national anthem, in which no animal is even mentioned? Don't make me laugh. Crow in stockinged feet would reach just above Colin Kaepernick's knee. That seemed like a good perspective on field exertions of any kind.

He wondered if, in other places, far away—on other planets like Venus, for instance—there wasn't even the idea of a leader because each creature would be its own leader, in fulfillment of its unique nature. An earthworm could look at a *hôtesse de l'air* without feeling inferior.

As if to justify all his suspicions, Crow made a discovery, and the result was a truly global beef on his part, something that threatened to turn him into a hate-all. It went like this:

Eagles, Cardinals, Seahawks, Falcons, Ravens, Hawks, Blackhawks, Blue Jays, Orioles, Raptors, Pelicans, Mud Hens, Chicks, Ducks, Penguins. That was just the beginning. Outside the professional teams there were Bantams, blackbirds, corsairs, chanticleers, gamecocks, pea hens, jayhawks, geese, and herons. Among others. No crows as animal avatars, a source of inspiration and identity among mates. No crow decorations on any T-shirts or key chains. No crows anywhere in that Costco full of licensing opportunities. No abstracted graphic symbol capable of being recognized by two-year-olds, who probably could barely see a field but could salute a banner because it would be hanging in their bedrooms, the test pattern of their emerging consciousness. No phrases, fight songs, or mottos capturing the inspirational quality of crows. ("Cheer, cheer for our squad of crows./ They sure know how to dodge all the blows./ They know every trick except/ the one that brings vic-to-ry!")

It got worse the deeper and wider you looked. Forget the Lions, Panthers, Bears, Rams, and Rays. No-brainers in a nasty, aggressive, competitive world. Ignore the bulldogs, badgers, beavers, and black squirrels. Horned frogs, Gila monsters, wombats, boll weevils, and even mad ants (!) all had a pop-mythic status somewhere in the sports world. Symbolically speaking, they were *visible*. They had a social-media presence and an audience. They resonated. They influenced.

Instead, tricky crows, thieving crows, scavenging crows, clever crows—none of these was a quality extolled by the broader society, not openly, even though all these qualities led to post-athletic success. When it came to birds, the world was ruled by nothing but rank hypocrisy. Crow knew a lot of birds who looked great when they were young and could really impress—plovers, for example, were underrated and could move their feet. Nobody fucked with pelicans. You just didn't. But old pelicans were about as pathetic as it gets, with their sagging, dragging beaks, their lack of options, and their dependency. They had no inner resources. Crow had seen too many of them hanging around small marinas in the south, content to be fed an occasional toss of offal by drunken tarpon fishermen. Instead, Crow scouted their favorite watering holes, bars with names like the Laff-a-Lot, Loons on a Limb, and Widdens, and stole watches and wallets just for the fun of it, just to see human beings freak out. Birds never freaked out. Panicked, yes, but never freaked out, never just lost it. It was one of the enduring pleasures of not being a person.

Colin Kaepernick never freaked out. Crow often wondered if he might actually be part crow somehow, despite his mad hair. He got royally screwed, got called far worse than any names Crow had ever heard, never stopped kneeling, and in the end got paid. He revealed all the owners, coaches, commissioners, power people, two thirds of his teammates, fans, broadcasters, television viewers, advertisers, people who drove cars or used grooming and physical-enhancement products to be exactly what they were: dupes. And terrified of the incontrovertible truth that they were.

So how could he still want that football thing? Rhetorical question. Crow knew. He'd flown over a field or two, seen how the simplicity of it, the pure green rectangle, abstracted reality, reduced the mess of experience and made it somehow intelligible. If you could handle the momentary fury and chaos, which Kaepernick seemed perfectly able to do. Quite likely, he had some sort of specialized vision, some freakish retinal capacity that enabled him to peer over the curvature of the Earth to spot his receivers. Crow could relate to that. Don't think, react. A pure world of unthought decisions, where actions spoke louder than words because there were no words, only cursing, grunting, phatic gestures of solidarity or hate. Take it easy, Crow, you're getting carried away. They were only cogs in a machine that ground up bodies and spit out money while people in front of screens fell asleep as if they had just had sex.

Still. And yet. Nevertheless. Crow had what the stiffs didn't have: access. He could land wherever he wanted, in almost any stadium he wanted. (Fuck domes! Domes are for pussies!) No turnstiles for him, no bag checks. He was on the field in San Francisco, in the Meadowlands, in Dallas when the roof was open. There was a hole in the roof (it was said) so God could watch His team play. Absolutely not. It was so Crow could shit on Jerry Jones' field and get away with it. But that felt too much like being a fan. Crow was famous for fifteen minutes when he landed on the dugout roof of Yankee Stadium on Opening Day just to hear the chatter and the cleats. ("Did you check out that club I told you about last night?" "It's hot as fuck today." "This pitcher's got nothing.") The ball boy came after him, the fan cam picked him up, and all the kids in the stadium started doing a modified crow hop in imitation. He saw it on the jumbotron. Ridiculous. Humiliating. Crow buzzed out of there like a shot and did a few dive-bombing swoops for effect. That was the last time Crow invaded commercial entertainment real estate (outside of a visit to Las Vegas).

That image on the jumbotron haunted Crow. This is what they all wanted, even Kaepernick: a mirrored version of themselves magnified by the confined space. To be empty of themselves and history, to become myth, living and battling between the quotation marks of cliché. And when—or if—they wanted to become mortal, get back in the flow, shed that aura of heightened reality? That possibility was already long foreclosed. Hercules didn't get to have a life, as Crow recalled. Back in the world meant nothing but gray days and ordinary madness, domestic strife, and unchannelable emotions. Quite apart from the medical bills. But no! Crow finally understood what Kaepernick had really done. When he knelt, he initiated his exit strategy. It was the first step in rendering himself voluntarily a creature of time, circumstance, and anonymity, as he had been born. He was practicing to become real.

And Crow? If for that moment in Yankee Stadium he had become the one crow, the image of crow, the idea of crow? He was already an egomaniac, and now this: jumbotron apotheosis. Shake that off, Crow. Go ahead and try. So ten thousand kids laughed at your image and hopped like ruptured ducks. It didn't matter why or even how you were famous. In your own head, you always would be, because you knew the Great American Truth that Colin Kaepernick had also embraced in his unique way: It is better to be pissed on than forgotten.

How could it have happened that Crow, of all creatures, could have been drawn in? In the first place, his sense of dissatisfaction was no greater than anyone else's. The sense of being too late, the sense that all the good things had been taken, the sense that life had passed him by (as they say), the sense of avoided responsibilities and, hence, missed opportunities. That was on him.

So where was the special sense of grievance, of doors closed in your face? Conspiracies, complots, and cabals? Crow didn't buy into any of that. Certainty enraged him. He did not suffer from body-image anxiety, and he didn't get messages telegraphed through his beak. He really couldn't believe it when he ran into a flock of cedar waxwings complaining darkly that no one had ever composed eclogues about them, that they never figured in anyone's mythology, and that this neglect was not accidental. Crow was no literati, but he hung out enough to quote at them: "I was the shadow of the waxwing slain/By the false azure in the windowpane." This was met with grudging silence, and some mumbling about the exception that proved the rule.

As a matter of fact, although cynical, Crow felt relatively secure in himself. He tested well. He didn't have unfulfilled desires, only proclivities. It was inconceivable that he would ever feel motivated to take on the entire world and seek to watch it burn.

Ah, but it is always those who think they know themselves so well who are the most susceptible, those who stand outside themselves always watching, who are surprised by revolutions of feeling that seem fomented from somewhere deep inside their own alien bodies. What Crow didn't know—did he?—was that something was missing, and that no story he had ever told about himself came close to filling it up.

Militants need the damaged ones, legions of them, the wronged. But they need even more the seekers who have stopped seeking, stopped because they have lost the ability and desire to imagine any realm beyond their own, just because they know it so well. Then, ah then, someone arrives to name that lack and fill that void.

Or perhaps Crow willed it unwittingly. Winter was coming, and Crow never migrated. But this time he decided to fly south on a whim, following wedges of ducks, grosbeaks, thrushes, and vireos. He picked them up, and they peeled off in Georgia, Florida, Mexico. He found himself alone in the mountains of Colombia and thought: What did I just do? But the jungle near Medellin was great, loaded with all kinds of stuff Crow had never tasted, like the larval stage of a blue morpho butterfly and some truly psychedelic fruits. Crow stuck out like a sore thumb among the splendid quetzals, parrots, macaws, and troupials of the edenic lowland forests. Not even so much as a "Where you from?" from any of them. It could have been a language thing, but the parrots looked haunted, and the migratorials only wanted to talk flyways and were already planning their trips north. It was a great climate, but they couldn't get back home fast enough. Crow loved the cool wetness, the water that seemed to come from everywhere, out of the air itself. He wanted to be part of the scene, but something told him to keep to himself. And that made him even more conspicuous.

He was roosting on the awning of Billares El Diamante, with its pool tables and old smokers, inside and out, when a thrush took a spot a bit too close to him. Crow nodded. Then thought he misheard: "Have you ever wondered how it would be if they weren't around?" Who? You mean *them*, like human beings? The ones who taught me how to bend twigs? The ones who leave me everything I value, everything that shimmers and shines? Crow thought of glass beads and squash blossom necklaces with bits of turquoise. You learn to take the bitter with the sweet.

But the thrush's rap was disturbingly simple and cut through all the compensatory pleasures: "You'll have to give that up, black boy, because they—all of them—want to do you harm. And not just you, you personally don't count, but all of us, all your brothers and sisters, as descended from the great age of reptiles. You know about that, right? No surprise if you don't because that would be the plan, to leave you ignorant of the time when we—you—ruled the earth. Velociraptors struck fear into everyone. Our ancestors. Believe it. They had *respect*. You probably don't know about the carrier pigeon either. An organized, meaningless wipe out. Genocide. And what about West Nile virus, you think that just sort of *happened*? You don't know about the secret government lab on Plum Island, Massachusetts? The Nile origin thing is just an Islamophobic cover."

The thrush clearly sensed Crow's skepticism, the skepticism of a city dweller, jaded, overly sophisticated, knee-jerk tolerant. But Crow knew, in his heart of hearts, birds of whatever feather were all dispensable, a kind of evolutionary cannon fodder, hastened by the pale penis people. The thrush looked at him hard.

"You don't have to believe a word I say. Just fly with me for a bit. No pressure, just a quick trip toward the coast."

What the heck, thought Crow, I've got nothing but time and a tour around might do me good.

They flew. Across the cordillera and down into the jungle along the Atrato River. From their perches they could see the open-pit gold mines like bald spots on a bushy head and trace the colorful plumes of pollution in the river. Even at a great height, the din of backhoes and bulldozers was shattering. In other parts of the jungle, they could hear gunshots, single and automatic. "Let's keep our distance," said the thrush. "It's not enough to take our homeland and burn the houses of the weaverbirds. They kill us for their sport." Crow saw one or two fall from the sky. He thought he had seen enough. The thrush didn't think so and steered them back toward Medellin. Crow arrived exhausted. He was having trouble breathing. The altitude was finally getting to him, but the thrush wouldn't let up. They came to a tall highway bridge on the far western outskirts of Medellin. Under the bridge he saw them, thousands of them: toucans, parakeets, thornbills, fiery topazes, and white-necked jacobins—refugees from everywhere, not just Antioquia but the whole country, the hemisphere, the continent. Thrush recited their names. Many of them huddled. They couldn't take the cold. Hawks that should have been killers were reduced to shivering bundles of feathers. In the vast mass, sudden disruptions flared, as incompatible species had finally had enough and tried to clear space. Feathers flew. Crow could see some bodies. He figured this kind of thing must be happening everywhere.

Thrush was talking quickly: "Millions on the move every

day. Displaced. Disappeared. Left alone, they'd die like dogs, pardon the reference. But enough of us understand what's happening, and we know we outnumber them. If we had hands and feet, we would already have taken over the world. Nothing to be done about that, but we've got eyes in the sky, condors that can cruise from here to Bogota, from here to Santa Marta. We know where they are weak: everywhere. We can wreck a gas station in minutes, just watch the movie. *The Birds*, that's our blueprint. Hitchcock was a genius. We can take down an airliner in seconds. There are a million gulls waiting to be martyrs. The cheeky ones in Bath who steal sandwiches right out of tourists' hands, they're practicing. Do I have to say anything about all the chickens raised in the bitterness of captivity? I could show you something else too, a group of shrikes that came all the way from South Africa just for the chance to fuck up the system. You know about them, Crow? They go harder than hard—pin their prey to fenceposts just for the fun of it. You think they are not looking forward to what's coming? After a few actions against a few high-value targets, anyone who is still sitting on the fence— excuse the metaphor—will join because they will see that not only can we win, we cannot be stopped. I mean birds don't care, we don't have feelings, we're animals, and animals don't back down. That's what they think, and we can use that. Like we can use you, Crow, you and all your kind. You're survivors. You're everywhere. You know how to adapt, and you're smarter than you look. But most of all nobody notices you anymore. You're like furniture or wallpaper. When they do notice you, they get the creeps, you scare them. Because they know you're watching them. Like that 'Nevermore' shit."

"That was a raven," Crow muttered, "sort of like a cousin with a totally fly wardrobe who is always trying to hit you up for something." It wasn't the first time he'd had to set someone straight about the stupid poem.

"Whatever. If you led a few well-placed attacks, high visibility, you know, like the steps of the Metropolitan, hit the tourists hard, they would freak their shit totally, and it would be ON. You look at me funny, Crow, but think about it. What are they going to do? They can't kill us all, we're the miner's canary if you know what I mean. We go down, they go down. Fucking insects would go crazy, and that would be it, like the *Hellstrom Chronicle* on steroids. They will have no choice; they will have to negotiate. And that's where you come in again. You have the smarts and the respect, nobody in the animal kingdom dislikes you, and in a year, you could be running the whole show. Yeah, there would be charismatic species that would be out front, like eagles and flamingos for eye candy, for the press, but you, Crow, could be calling the shots, making policy, changing the fucking world. What do you say? Are you in?"

Without looking at the bird, just listening to his voice, Crow could imagine what was possible: millions of human deaths, a war to end all wars. Habitats were at stake, the livability of the entire planet, at least as far as birds were concerned. Human beings were the problem; they had to go. What if he could end all that? Clean slate.

And then what? A brave new world? One for all and all for one? More like hawks and sparrows. He'd seen a red-tailed hawk treat Central Park like it was a personal no-fly zone. That would never change no matter what battles they fought together. Likewise, Crow had never made it long term with a representative of any other species, even when they showed him some leg. Not the scarlet tanagers or the orioles that he imagined would be nice. Crow always thought it was social, but he knew, really, it went deeper than that. It was the nature of things that kept them all apart and even made some of them perpetual enemies. Fucking shrikes. Fucking osprey.

Crow finally looked at the thrush. His eyes were glassy, and his beak was smacking, like when an old-fashioned tape runs out and the reels keep turning.

"You know what, I'm gonna head back," said Crow. "Seems like you have it worked out, so I'll just fend for myself."

The thrush backed away, measuring him. "I think you need time to get your head around it. Stay a few more days above the billiard parlor. It will all be clear. And you should meet my *compañera* Maria Luz. She is a seriously hot saffron finch. I think she'd like you." Then he added, "I love you, Crow, but come the revolution, you'll be the first to go. There's no room for the uncommitted. That's as bad as being on the other side. Worse."

Crow took off that night after watching two old men play a game of eight ball that lasted two hours. They wore the same moth-eaten sweaters and drank coffee from small cups balanced on the table rail. They tried impossible shots that never worked. They seemed to enjoy nothing more than regarding the intricate combinations of color and number on the green field of the table, modified with every stroke. They had infinite patience and good humor. Time felt like an illusion. One of them noticed Crow watching from outside. He took off his pinky ring and placed it on the edge of the table next to his coffee cup, as an invitation. It glinted. Crow nodded in appreciation.

Crow flew back toward the North. He watched his back the whole way.

There were no billiard parlors that he could find in New York, but he kept looking, with the memory of that one in Medellin as his guide.

15. Crow in Cities

What was Crow's job? Was it to eat, to steal, and to make more Crows? Or was it, instead, to see, to describe, to sweep up whatever was in the path of his eye, to embrace an absolute idiocy of registration that could match the city's being. To exalt being in the city and to glorify nothing because it is not needed. A new kind of beauty exalts itself, uses all being to realize itself. Crow knew this as if it were a message he had hacked from a primitive flip phone.

Beyond the beyond, at the inlet dividing Brooklyn and Queens, Crow felt lost in endless reticulations of a highway that followed contours having nothing to do with direction or destination. He made a snake's progress through a vast undulating cemetery, a city that doubled and distorted the silver city he could barely see across the water in Manhattan. But that one was perfectly vertical and pure, a light space modulator, built to gather light, hold it until the very last instant of the day and transmit it here, to the stunted city of decaying monuments and nonliving things, the outlying boroughs where Crow lived.

Crow felt time stop in the meandering rows of untended tombs and headstones. The thoroughfares were crowded with sepulchral houses of granite and limestone, more ambitious for status than houses of the living, as if the afterlife itself could not be trusted to provide. Names and dates festooned everything. Some were rubbed out by weather, and others may have been left blank because the stone carver had not been paid or the owner sought to put off the end date and the tomb itself was still vacant. Crow's life had no record; it was radically unbracketed.

Many stones had small enamel portraits blanked by exposure to the weather or perhaps waiting for an image. Spirit pictures?

Across the water nothing died, nothing was born in that metallic light. On this side of the river, it was a city of cemeteries. There were others on hills in the distance he could barely make out. Obelisks, temples, and palaces in smokey light, ancient in their references, and doubly dead if you thought about it. It didn't bother Crow that the entire region had been given over to the dead, who no longer cared how much land they had or who came to visit. And were never late. Like Crow. As far as he was concerned, they had no presence at all because they had never lived, and so were not in the least dead. Cemeteries were like books whose bindings disdained their contents. Remembrance was not his thing.

A small child in an absurdly long coat did a sideways crabwalk run among the stones, laughing like a maniac as her parents tried to catch her. Sonya, they called her. Crow identified.

He lifted off over Brooklyn into barely defined zones of industrial noise, where things were being unmade and built back up. Piles, deposits, collections, lots, yards, parking areas, fencing, razor wire, chain link, shipping containers in half a dozen colors all rimmed with red rust. They were stacked everywhere in forgotten and unexpected places, near the water but not close to any dock or ship, under bridges, laid end to end along the interior roadways of parks. Crow never saw them opened, emptied, or moved, yet overnight they might disappear.

Fenced off or standing open in defiance of pilfering were bundles of paving stones, 4 x 6 beams, PVC tubing, and concrete pipe, naked or wrapped in blue or green plastic tarps. In some places, the material had sat for years without being used, waiting to be joined with other heavy elements in a campaign against entropy.

A losing battle even in the short run, with the evidence everywhere, in the cracked and buckling pavement, the sagging asphalt and gaping holes, the out-of-the-way streets with no sidewalks or curbs that disappeared under water when it rained. In the trash-filled alleys between buildings. Crow wandered, Crow was *drawn* to these passages, where he immersed himself in the smell of rot and the sounds of someone playing the flute from a high window and a couple fighting energetically, each phrase punctuated with the crash of dishes hurled through a window and down to the pavement. Duck, Crow! The insults were in Russian, Polish, Yiddish, Chinese, Creole, Wolof, Italian, Hindi. Crow could not speak any of them. It was like someone had placed a knife across his beak to keep him quiet.

Crow wandered. That was his job. He also understood what birds who stayed at home, spent their time in parks and backyards never had an inkling: This city was water. Crow's earliest memory was not the green of trees or the beak of the mother but light on water, scattering with the current into a thousand splinters. "Those who remain and wave are unaware." A poet's line that stuck with him, as only poets' lines can do. As for the gulls, pelicans, and terns, they never came close to town unless it was to pick over trash, so how could they know? Beach bums. They could never appreciate water the way he could because it was their wallpaper, their white noise. Terrestrial, Crow could sense all the better where the water wanted to go, how it penetrated every part of the sclerotic concrete cover, driven by a tidal gravity. He could feel the movement under the houses of Park Slope and the apartments of Red Hook, into the subway tunnels and sub-basements of downtown's half-empty skyscrapers. He followed the short meander of the Gowanus Canal, past the barges and cranes of metal recyclers, under bridges with clattering wooden roadways and rusting bridgetender's cabins, flanked by shiny new buildings built too close to the water, money's victory against logic and experience, with esplanades that gave strollers a perfect view of the noxious, bilious olive sludge. There were sunken ships, oil cans, and canoes. This was his Brooklyn. Crow rejoiced!

As Crow followed the canal toward its outlet near vacant docks and empty storage yards, he liked to imagine—if that's the right word for someone with a limited sense of history—what it all once was. He could see in his mind's eye the looming bulk of the container ships and freighters filling the shoreline. They unloaded and loaded from the rail tracks that snaked everywhere among the vast industrial buildings nearby. In the entrance shed to the docks, a squat man, there to control the traffic and deliveries, watched the sailors and stevedores cross the street directly to the corner bar, Sunny's or Hank's Saloon or the Flag, something like that, where they tended to stay until the sky turned from red to dark blue and the lights came on and the stars came out, and they never bothered to sign out at the shed and wouldn't bother to sign in in the morning because that would already be taken care of. The cobblestones glistened in the streetlights.

Sunny's. If Crow were a drinker, it would have been his place. Now all the cobblestones were paved, and the piers were caged with chain link as they rotted. Nubs of pilings, green with slime, stuck up from the water like growth in a cypress swamp. Crow landed on the asphalt stretch of one forlorn pier. He gazed out at the Statue of Liberty, which looked dented. He noticed that grass was growing through cracks in the rubbery pavement. That cheered him up momentarily.

Crow noted customs, movements, shifts. He saw commuters standing weary and defeated at the subway hole. Others passed along the streets, looking up, anxious, blank, remembering. Rats scurried and hid. He flew through a forgotten park, past a ruined empty stadium. A family dressed in bright summer colors that contrasted with the deep blackness of their skin sat alone in the broken bleachers watching several men in immaculate whites play a game of cricket. The ground was lumpy with stones, spiked with glass, and green only with weeds. They could have been on the moon. He perched himself on a light pole and watched one single corner of the street. A man in a USPS uniform and shorts passed by and stumbled on the curb. Later—how much later?—another man in another uniform, a different one, also in shorts, stumbled on the same corner. Crow suspected this was not coincidence but some deep regularity that only his indolence could discover. A couple noticed Crow and stared at him for a long time. Crow stared back. He didn't turn his head.

Crow watched the passage from day to night, night back to day. All around him the borough felt silver and brittle blue. The concrete in shadow turned black while the windows of the new towers, now encroaching on his side of the river, multiplied the clouds and sky like screens of a fragmented movie. The action was all up above and mirrored down below. Huge tufts of clouds piled up in the distance. Crow waited for what happened next. Crow didn't trust blue days, with their aching uninflected clarity. Disasters happened on blue days. He would wait them out, the falling towers, the inundated streets, the parks livid with distempered racoons. He would keep his eyes on the nocturnal animals and the tidal rhythms, on stratocumulus smudges, contrails, and the shadings of yellow and gray until they deepened into the orange evenings of September. No matter what the apocalypse, this was Crow's place.

He was gripped by the elation of witnessing a spectacle intended for no one.

16. Crow and Phoenix
(for Xu Bing)

In a triumph of hope over experience, Crow flew to Phoenix. As much as Crow appreciated the subtleties of the desert, he had never had any desire to visit Phoenix. He knew it primarily by reputation for its golf courses. The Raven course would probably have been just right for someone like him, intrigued as he was by nuanced greens. No greens fees or membership vetting for Crow, no embarrassment about a high handicap. The brutal temperatures, especially in midsummer, did not deter him because he didn't have to worry about dropping his keys in the parking lot and suffering instant heatstroke. But he was leery of other, unspoken appeals, to another Crow deep inside him, one who wore orthopedically friendly white shoes and complained full time about the government and free handouts to the undeserving.

And there was the decimated water table. So no, Crow had no plans to follow the great southern migration of Lexuses, Cadillacs, and Mercedes out of the Midwest in late November.

Still, he went. What could have induced him? A purely rhetorical question, given that the author certainly knows the answer. It was the sudden awareness of irreconcilable opposites—the sky above, the mud below—that provoked a longing deep inside for the unifying power of myth. The name itself held such a promise: Phoenix, immortal creature heaped in the lore of the extraordinary. Everything in Crow's world had become so familiar, so toneless. Day to day, he endured a background sense that everything was already remembered and soon to be forgotten. Nothing ventured, nothing gained/Nothing sacred or profane—a ditty he couldn't shake. Phoenix reminded him that the world hadn't always been ordinary.

Crow was raised on myth and fable, legend and bald-faced lies that were too good to be true and too true to be dismissed. They were the gift of parents who should have known better. The body of a dead kingfisher could point toward threatening weather. A special stone found in the nests of certain swallows could enable the blind (of any sort) to see. Peacocks were so vain, they could not bear to stare at their own feet. (Crow didn't pay a lot of attention to those parts either.) Auks accompanied pharaohs on their way to the underworld. The hoopoe slept all winter long like a bat, dreaming of warmth and learning patience from bears. Pelicans would peck their own breasts to feed their children on blood. Once long ago, Crow believed them, or wanted to. Above all was the phoenix.

The immortal creature thrilled him with horror and wonder. It fed on incense pearls, knew of its own end before it arrived, and set fire to its nest in anticipation. The ashes of its auto-da-fé were stored with myrrh and carried to a new nest for re-birth. (Carried by whom?) Crow had heard other versions, but the outline was consistent. The world began when a primordial mound rose from the sea and the phoenix bird landed on it. Its cry was the first sound ever heard. (Again, by whom?) Its feathers contained all five colors, and its body represented the six celestial bodies: The eyes were the sun, the head was the sky, the wings were the wind, the back was the moon, the tail the planets, and the feet were the Earth. So some Chinese believed, and who was Crow to say different? There was a connection to the Milky Way, but Crow couldn't remember what it was.

The main thing about all these legends was that a bird wasn't just a bird, but always also something else, linked to the astral plane. No chromosomal map or genealogical tree offered up by the ornithologists could ever compare with dining on incense pearls.

At the moment of deepest need, his universe untuned, Crow decided to go to Phoenix.

Low and ungainly, with a generic downtown, the city spread among tufts of green toward the Sonoran Desert. Crow ignored the golf courses, their fairways turning brown, watering systems down to a trickle. He followed the growth corridor past the mobile home and RV parks of Casa Grande, where paint was peeling and metal siding warping in the sun. Up ahead, lots were already marked out, and hookups were in, waiting for elderly climate refugees from Michigan, Minnesota, Wisconsin, and points north. A sign read: "Fastest growing community in America. If you lived here, you'd be home by now." Tucson shimmered like a mirage somewhere at the Earth's edge.

Making his aerial rounds, Crow met a flock of white-crested sparrows already ensconced in a patch of shrub. He barely recognized them. They seemed to have shed their brown and grey coats for radiant pastels and an occasional plaid. It made their crests only seem whiter. "You must be boiling in that," one of them said. Another added, "That's why we have consignment shops. I don't miss my tweeds and sweaters, not for minute. We're a little more causal down here. You'll probably want a new wardrobe." A third one said, "The newcomers club meets tonight. You should come. Swell folks. By the way, we also have singles events."

You profess disappointment, Crow, with your fantastical expectations? What were you thinking?

No longer dreaming of renewal, Crow rocketed toward the sun. He saw a feather drop from his tail. It spiraled down and down, like a plunging helicopter, toward a recycling yard somewhere between Mesa and Tempe. The yard bordered a narrow river with a mountain of discarded metal, protruding girders, and fragments of stoves, grills, refrigerators, and aluminum siding. So much for civilization, Crow thought, as he watched his own feather land near an insect-like crane that was lifting tangled buckets from the mountain of junk and depositing them in battered containers. Where would they go after that? Into an infernal mine deep in the earth, where creatures, half mole, half human, would render them back into their primordial elements? Crow was mesmerized by the mechanical fauna, but he was even more concerned with finding that feather.

Crow had never lost a feather before, except under extreme duress. He refused to accept that it was one more step toward decrepitude and sartorial regression. Those pastels. He was willing to risk everything to retrieve this piece of himself and preserve his blackness. He descended into the din of the yard. Something was going on there that brought him up short to perch on the suddenly motionless crane. An empty pickup truck had pulled into the middle of the yard, and instead of depositing, it was retrieving. Crow watched with interest as a short Chinese man and a crew of teenagers—they seemed like characters from an anime game—combed through the tangled piles and threw pieces into the back of the truck until it was so full it could barely move. It took only a few minutes, and off they went. Crow found another perch on a nearby office shed to wait for his opportunity to retrieve the missing black bit of himself and fell into the rhythm of the crane, scooping and dropping, scooping and dropping.

An hour later they were back again with an empty truck, and they repeated the routine. Crow tried to discover a pattern in the things they chose but couldn't, even though they seemed to be very particular. Crow flashed on nesting behavior, and it suddenly became obvious that this crew was building something. The idea of something taking form in the midst of all this entropic surplus, this apocalyptic trash heap, got to him. It felt poignant and futile, as hopeless as his trying to preserve a lost feather. The mad buildup, the heedless sprawl, the continuous collapse and replacement as pointless as a hamster in a wheel cage, with the same endpoint—utter exhaustion—that was the direction of things. But the sun didn't care about birds or beauty or bailed wire. It pounded everything on a glowing anvil. *Carajo*, it was hot! Okay, he got it about the pastels. But these Asian recyclers, they must be mad or know something. Crow decided to follow them.

The truck banged along past half-empty strip malls and out along a dirt road that led to a decaying industrial park. In the corner was a long corrugated shed, festooned with paper banners carrying messages in Chinese characters. Somewhere on his family tree, Crow was sure he had Asian cousins; he wished they were here. Next to the shed was a growing heap of scrap metal. A steady stream of kids went back and forth ferrying pieces into the shed. He overheard one of the teenagers say, "This is the last fucking internship I sign up for. They warned me about the University of Phoenix."

The shed was open at either end, so Crow swooped in to take a look and landed in the rusty rafters. Below him, something was putting itself together. There were ten people in helmets at work with welding torches. The man from the truck directed them. He was dressed like a college professor. The heat was hellish, undiminished by a battery of electric fans. They were working on the truncated torso of something vaguely dragonlike, spread out on the floor to gigantic length. It was composed of everything from car exhaust pipes and roofing tin to pipe wrenches. The pieces looked to Crow not just forlorn but devastated, as if an entire civilization had exploded and vanished, leaving its litter behind. Each piece bore the traces of its previous world that no longer was. If you started throwing away perfectly good pipe wrenches, what was next?

Crow didn't have to be a genius to see in the wreckage a prophecy. This must be why Phoenix existed, as a laboratory of folly, an air-conditioned nightmare errand into the wilderness, herald of an unlivable future.

And yet, something was putting itself together, which was really why Crow was here. Fit together into the form of a giant—yes, it must be a bird, the only bird it could be—each piece lost its sadness, forgot its damaged past. Nothing was repaired, but everything was cashed in, brought back, liberated, and reconvened. Redeemed in glory. Seeing the thing come together as the welders worked, Crow longed for such a transmogrification of his own shabby self, an inner blowtorch capable of liquifying his rigid attitudes and melding all the disparate memories and impulses into a singular soul, finite but unbounded. Beware of mysticism, Crow, beware of beauty's false promise of unity and the end to all questions. Beware of taking the part for the whole, beware of banners and anything written on them. Beware of exhortations. Beware of magical thinking and deus ex machina solutions. Do not swoon or surrender to metaphor. You are in the very world, Crow, which is the world of all of us, the place in which we find our happiness, or not at all.

Did Crow listen to his inner admonitions? The welders worked. The interns from the University of Phoenix—immaterial but real—complained. The heat rose. The phoenix took outline. Crow saw the man from the truck, the boss, the professor, the artist, whatever he was, take something from his pocket and tape it to the wing of the giant creation. It was the feather he had lost. Crow hunkered down. He was prepared to wait for the moment of vitality he knew would come, and the power of flight, animated wholly from within. No motors, no batteries, no USB ports, but perhaps some divine energy from that lost feather of his. When the thing lifted off, metal plumage flashing in the sun, Crow would climb with it as living symbol, leaving behind a world whose destruction was imminent and whose rebirth was uncertain.

Crow built his nest in the air, constructed it of illusions as brittle as sticks. Yet, in spite of his reputation as an aesthete, even as someone with a forbiddingly abstract sense of the world, Crow's dirty secret was that he was a thoroughgoing materialist.

He wasn't born that way. It snuck up on him. It wasn't just the failed revolutions, the stale sense he always felt that hovered around the question: So, what's really different after all? That was just garden-variety disillusion, adolescent, like freaking out that the wings of your beloved were turning from black to brown to white. Surprise at anything, least of all the body's insurgencies, struck him as a total failure of consciousness. But this was something different, more global, less personal. How to chart it, like an illness?

Crow felt that long ago, when he was young, time had stopped so that stories could begin. He told himself stories about everything, about how it all began (the first egg, cosmic, born from a star that had lost its light), about where it was going (toward pure flight, becoming all wing, never to touch down again), who was to blame if it didn't happen (raptors, humans, unimaginable predators), and best of all, how crows alone came to know the secrets at the heart of things. That universe was alive in the telling. It vibrated with meaning. All things might change, every particular object could disappear, but the form remained, like the smile of a Cheshire cat (excuse the simile, Crow). It was immanent, a glittering image in the mind's eye of all crows, and Crow shared it and sang it and lorded it over all other creatures who just couldn't see the larger truth. Pathetic, really, how could they move, love, endure another day, without such an image to justify them?

And then one day Crow met the owl.

Met is maybe the wrong word. It was, to borrow a phrase, a cold day in hell, and Crow happened to be up past his bedtime searching for someplace to hunker down out of the deep freeze. He remembered once seeing sparrows in the woods flock around a human being like a cloud, just to gain warmth. That would never work for him. Too much size inspiring too much fear. Around sparrows, Crow felt like a clinking, clanking caliginous clod. But the cold made Crow feel enormous sympathy for all living things. It allowed him to feel what wretches feel, and, at a deeper level, that only confirmed his dark celebration.

But Crow met the owl.

It sat high up in a beech tree, the orange-brown leaves hanging off the branches like paper flags. There was no better place than a forest in winter, if it weren't for the cold. The owl was dressed for it, in a thick coat that made him seem twice his size. Before Crow could say anything, the owl blinked and said, "Don't even think about stopping here. You'll interrupt me while I'm working." Crow was about to ask a question, but the owl read his bird-thought: "I kill."

Crow mused out loud, "I've never killed, not exactly, not anything major, only worms and insects. I could have, I'm not above it, after all, but it's hard for me to –"

The owl cut him off. "The first time I killed a field mouse I almost barfed. It was electric with fear, pure instinctual dread. I told myself not to think. Just follow an inclination, pay attention to my nature. I crushed it to near pulp and swallowed it whole." The owl never deigned to look at Crow, only stared straight ahead, blinking occasionally, preternaturally focused on the gathering darkness. "I looked into myself and found what I was ordained to do."

Crow thought, this is how the world divides: killers by nature and everyone else. He remarked, "The parable of the scorpion and the turtle: an appeal to nature by someone who has abdicated responsibility for choosing."

Crow's glib existential formulation obviously annoyed the bird, and Crow interpreted the weird twisting of its head as a gesture of disapproval. "I know all about that sanctimoniousness, and it doesn't suit you, Crow. You're happy to let birds like me do your killing for you, and if there's a leftover, an accursed share, that's where you come in." Not that you ever leave much, Crow thought. The owl continued to scan the evening terrain, to no outcome. "Look, with you here I'm obviously not going to have much luck tonight, although luck is a meaningless concept when it comes to what I'm up to."

Crow was certainly not naïve about how the world worked, and being on the periphery of the food chain gave him perspective on the role of violence in the social system of the so-called animal kingdom. But meeting a killer with a developed sense of irony left him momentarily speechless, although this one laid it on a little thick. And in spite of his working knowledge of owls, Crow didn't entirely trust the raptor. But Crow was cold, and the bigger bird cut the draft. He felt okay about his chances.

"What is it you do, exactly?" asked the owl.

"Honestly?" Crow asked. "I tell stories. About what I find,

how things look, where they come from, where they end up, and what it all means. Two cups stuck in a fence, some bent venetian blinds, bottle caps from three different craft beers from three different continents. Why so many different beers in so many different places? I weave theories. I speculate."

The owl appeared to ponder while doing nothing. "An anecdoted typography of chance is not a system, not a theory, not a narrative. How about something a little more germane, like an explanation for this evening's erratic behavior among the mammals of the field? I consider myself something of an expert in pattern recognition, and I don't see the underlying relevance in what you say. A little more attention to the facts on the ground might suit you better. But I am willing to play along, since I've got nothing better to do. I'll tell you a few things about me, and you make up a story."

Crow thought, my goal here should not be to tell the truth but to be convincing. Crow also thought, if I am not convincing, or at least diverting, there might be consequences. Facts on the ground.

The owl let out in fairly rapid succession: "I once picked up a truck. I attacked a fisherman and took out his eye. I kept it until it dried out, then I ate it. I don't actually like the moon, but I'm used to it. Contrary to popular belief, it doesn't help my work. The thing I like least about me? My reputation as a bird of ill omen, but it can be useful. You know a little bit about that, Crow, don't you? Gender-wise, you can't pin me down. The laughing owl is not extinct; it simply stopped laughing. There's more I could add, of course."

Owl gave Crow a collection of anecdotes, a verbal scrapbook

covered with bird tracks, flecked with blood. Crow thought, now that I've seen the way things are, I discover that this materialist, this death-dealing master of facts, is the worst kind of romantic. He wants his fortune told. He wants to imagine his own apotheosis. What does a fortune teller do? Takes what you know about yourself and gives it back to you, minus the trauma. And the message is always the same: You have a future, you win. Crow didn't think that would work in this case. It would have to be something darker, more titanic, a tale that asserted that all that had happened everywhere up to now conspired to make this bird what, who, and where he is. Cosmic destiny on a tree limb, unfolding before the beginning of time, a context fit for creatures who believed they had seen it all.

This put Crow in a new relation to his own idiom, to the yarns he spun as naturally as breathing. Crow realized that you don't need to suffer in order to sing the blues. You just have to be a good musician. You don't have to believe your stories (although, nostalgically, he could see how that might help); you just need the right words in the right places, and let the listeners do the rest. Crow the evangelist become the cynical bard? Or was there left a joy in ultimate risk before an audience with insatiable need and infinitesimal patience? Crow collected himself and commenced: "There was war in heaven, and the winged angels were separated into two . . ."

18. Crow Contra Darwin

Crow often thought to himself: It really is like they say it is. Isn't it? He knew the basic drill without a lot of counter-intuitive cladistic finagling. He had seen it in action plenty of times. Nature threw a lot of stuff against the wall, and some of it stuck. And it kept sticking until it didn't. And threw some more stuff, and some of that stuck. And so on and so forth, getting somewhere or other, eventually. That was evolution. The "eventually" was, for all practical purposes, him. But where was that? He felt that he had not stuck to the wall very firmly and could be easily dislodged. He certainly didn't feel like a winner. Perhaps all of his kind was in the same leaky boat, but he couldn't worry about them.

To ask the question again: Where had he—or his kind—got to over the eons? He assumed it was eons, since everybody talked that way, referring to the ancient past where nothing anyone said could be fully checked out, much less referred to first-person eyewitness testimony. Exactly nowhere, he suspected, with everyone and everything as short term as the next cataclysmic event. A big meteor would do it, but probably you didn't need that. A global forest fire, a month of really bad smog days? Peel back the whole survival-of-the-fittest bromide and you could see how nugatory and uninspiring the whole thing was. Who's fit enough to take on an asteroid? On the one hand—Hollywood reference coming up here—"still the same old story, a fight for love and glory." On the other hand, persisting and persisting, heading nowhere but sustained by some miniscule genetic advantage. Standing in for his entire species, Crow felt he pretty much had every available advantage and couldn't imagine what would give him even more of an edge. Blacker wings? Not in most parts of the country. A longer beak? Crow was already the butt of jokes on that front. ("How come crows have such long noses? So they can eat out of the corner of a box.") A better singing voice? Maybe, but that would take a while, and he, personally, wouldn't be around to benefit.

That was the crunch, the psychological dead end that led to faulty philosophical reasoning. What good was evolution if he, the only Crow, the one unique being and the only entity he could truly know, could not directly experience the benefit of it in his lifetime and know that if he wanted to, he could pass it on? Who cared about contemplating the rest of creation from the top of some demographic pyramid? Worse than that, no matter how well you learned how to master the local scene, the biome and its vagaries, that only made you more of an idiot in the face of change, a Blockbuster Video franchise of the animal kingdom. No need to preach organizational nimbleness to Crow. He'd kibbitzed on some Ted Talks in front of demo monitors in the window of the nearby Best Buy. (How much longer would it be around?) It would be better to wake up and find that at least you could do covers of Billy Joel and Bruce Springsteen, or maybe even Smokey Robinson, best case scenario. That was evolution you could believe in. And with that mad skill, you really would feel invincible and eternal, like you could survive the separation of the continents or even a meteor crash.

This explains why Crow had never been especially impressed or even convinced by the story he had heard—that most birds loved to repeat, over and over—that they had descended from dinosaurs. Everybody talked about the dinosaurs: "Nobody has-sled T-Rex!" "Raptors ruled!" "Just goes to show that we were here first." Crow's response was, "What do you not understand about the word 'descend'? It means to go down. To get worse. To be second rate." And he would add, "I don't see any dinosaurs among us, do you? Anyone get that kind of respect? Bald eagles? Really? Don't make me laugh. How about the respect a shark gets? Or a coral snake, or even a scorpion?" This kind of talk made him tremendously unpopular. He tried to keep his beak shut and avoid the worst provocations. It made Crow feel that, somehow, he had been reverse engineered to be a curmudgeon.

This attitude amounted to a form of paranoia, a conviction that things could, in fact, run backward. Over time, you could slough off features and attributes if you didn't need or use them, toes for example, or even wings. He'd seen—well, no, he had heard of—giant birds that couldn't fly at all, the emu and the os-trich. How was that an advantage? How was it an adaptive strat-egy? Penguins he could sort of see. But losing your wings just so you could run fifty miles an hour? How did such an embar-rassment even happen? Crow imagined running like hell over the desert, trying to get off the ground, knowing that whatever feline predator was chasing you, the chances were good that they would win and you would lose. Nobody had to tell Crow that nature was a zero-sum game. The idea that such thwarted things could exist, that they somehow *over* adapted in an orgy of specificity, revealed to Crow that nature was more deeply per-verse than he had imagined.

But the emu and the ostrich pointed Crow elsewhere, toward hitherto unsuspected possibilities, strange folds in nature's continuous surface. What if they weren't so funny or pathetic or outmoded? What if they were a herald of things to come? In his mind's eye, Crow saw the reverse future unfold, the deeper scenario of de-evolution, the pattern behind apparent confusion. The problem was that no one had been around long enough to grasp the big picture. The ice would melt; the seas would rise. Volcanoes would increase. Global travel would be canceled. Various airlines would go under. Primordial conditions would return. Crow would lose his feathers and even his wings. As they shrank, they would begin to morph into small but effective forearms with sharp claws. Likewise, his head would tilt, his tail lengthen, his jaws elongate and expand, and the tyrannosaurus that sill resided somewhere deep within him would be back. Human beings would be but one power among many powers, if they were lucky. A new (old) age would begin. And then . . . And then . . .

19. Crow Experiences Unreality and Appeals to Ram Dass for a Solution

Crow had always felt a certain sense of unreality, as if he were wrapped in swaddling up to his eyeballs and looked out on the world like some kind of spy, or less than that, like a passerby. He was puzzled by everything he saw but lacked the interest to probe it, query it, wrest new meanings from his experience. It was a little like being a zombie or a ghost, in it but not of it, there but not there. Crow had always chalked this up to an avian problem, but was it?

Crow heard the sound of gunfire in the distance. All the birds around him scattered, and the larger creatures of the field, the charismatic megafauna—the deer, bear, coyotes, and foxes—took off. Crow was mildly fascinated to watch a bear run, a kind of propelled waddle that gained such incredible momentum that the animal had trouble stopping. The guns kept sounding, a pointed pop pop pop that seemed to drift on the air. Sounds that had no consequence, something from far away carried to Crow's hearing like a rumor.

He could see the men with rifles. Every now and then, one would catch a glint of light. For that instant they seemed almost real. But Crow didn't believe in them, or if he did, the problem was, he felt absolutely nothing. He searched himself for fear and found nothing, no emotion at all. Courage and cowardice (it has often been remarked) can have the same appearance in the act of doing nothing. Crow did nothing. He watched as the men with the guns drew closer to his perch, where he was obviously exposed.

They were there, he was here, and he felt these two realities could never be connected, in any world. They could never reach across the chasm that separated whatever was real about them (to themselves) and what was uniquely real to him, that is, his swaddled self. Even the pellets of a shotgun shell were impossible. To reach him, they would first have to travel half the distance, and to do that, they would first have to travel half that distance, and to do that, they would first have to travel half that distance, and so on until they were frozen in some infinitesimal microsecond of complete stasis. Besides, Crow wasn't a game bird. He was just biological interference. Why would anyone not a farmer shoot at him?

Because he was *there*. Here. In the arena. The spray of pellets ripped through the branches above his head. He still didn't move. He realized that this sense of the world's unreality was the source of his insane belief in his own invincibility. Like his native namesake, Absaroka, the Crow Indians, whose vision quests gave them special powers, especially in battle. But not on the material plane. Better to have it all hard wired, like an antelope or a giraffe. You get wind of a lion, and you take off, no hesitation, no strategizing, no if-this-then-that, no feelings of nameless dread. Just pure adrenaline and speed, and the winner depends on the luck of the genetic draw. No celebrating when you outrun the latest, greatest predator. Likewise, no regrets when the lion gets his chompers on your throat. Just an uncomprehending departure. One minute you were there, and the next minute you weren't. How was that any different from a fly snapped up by a frog's tongue? It's a jungle out there, a flat landscape of men with guns and not a Great Chain of Being with cerebral Crow at the top. And speaking of lions, Crow had taken advantage of the remains of more than a few downed ruminants. He had once admired the performance of a big cat hanging a buffalo hide in a tree, though he couldn't for any earthly reason see the purpose. Later, he wasn't above taking a sample. It was worse than jerky.

But this was Crow's basic problem: He should have been on the wing, and instead he was wool-gathering, pondering abstractions.

The next spray of pellets caught the tip of his wing. A flesh wound, some feathers, a bagatelle. The problem now became what to do. If he moved, he'd be even more visible. If he didn't, they would probably just shoot again in his general direction and might get lucky. He could drop to the ground and play dead, but the dog they had with them would probably chew him up just for fun. Dogs were so craven they would do anything for a little human affection. Crow's only choice at this point was to go with his own passivity. No sense fighting against your nature. Be Here. Now. Crow hunkered down. The hunters were only yards from the tree. The stupid Irish setter was barking up a storm.

"Crows are just flying rats as far as I'm concerned. Why waste another shell on something we can't stick in our bag. Target practice is over," the hunters said. "Besides, fucking bird's already dead and just doesn't know it. Take a look at its sorry ass up there."

Flying rats? That was a pigeon epithet. Sorry ass? Yeah, they'd be looking a little mussed if somebody opened up on them with heavy weapons. Crow, the bird of peace, would not be provoked. On the other hand, "Already dead and just doesn't know it"? For Crow, the thought was worse than being shot. It was the abyss itself. Will I know it when I'm dead? If not, if I can't know *that*, the most important thing, then all this really is unreal, a prelude to nothing. Maybe nothing more than a dream dreamed in Sicily by a goat asleep in the sun. And if it is unreal, how can I possibly know that, without anything to measure it against but more unreality?

The hunters had long since moved off, the threat level dialed back from red to pale yellow, but Crow was still there, pondering how a goat might dream. Still insulted, still thinking.

Crow was no student of history, which made his dream of the atomic age all the more surprising to him. Although, when he considered it, he had to admit that the atomic age was not finished by any means, and, therefore, he himself was a part of it, like it or not. There were centrifuges. There was toxic-site remediation. There was the concept of nuclear winter. There were abrogated nonproliferation treaties. The dream must have come out of some deep foreboding.

Crow didn't see the signs plastered all over the chain-link fence warning him (not him, of course, but curious and unauthorized bipeds) to stay clear of the restricted testing area. It was a desert, after all, and deserts were Crow's second home. He loved deserts for their clarity, nuance, and noncommittal weather. Ten feet of desert was worth more to him than a hundred acres of any mountain he'd ever been on. Drawn to shimmering dunes, he flew on, heedless of the craters that pockmarked the desert floor.

The blast caught him by surprise. It was a silent flash in the far distance, and Crow was thinking about real-estate prices at the instant. By the time a wave of sound hit him, he was already blinded by a light that turned the blue sky above him black, like a photographic negative. (Crow had seem them in various trash heaps.) The heat was intense, batting him around in midair like a tennis racket. It seemed to go on forever, and Crow thought he was dead, followed by the realization that he couldn't be dead or he wouldn't be having thoughts at all.

Crow found himself alone under a towering cloud. His whole

body tingled, painfully alive and raw. Plucked. Crow looked at his wings and found that most of the feathers had disappeared. What he could see of his tail was a singed stump. He was nothing but a vibrating nerve, and the pain was tremendous, although it seemed more theoretical than actual. Crow attempted to fly, but without feathers it was impossible. He was forced to walk across fields of fused glass and ash. In the distance, he saw vehicles populated by people in hazmat suits. When they approached him, he found it impossible to flee, just as he found it impossible to resist when they gathered him into a sealed container coated with lead. He was radioactive! Crow knew that that meant his chances of even short-term survival were nil.

Nevertheless, they deposited him in a substantial but antiseptic holding facility—don't call it a cage—and seemed intent on studying him, a temporary survivor. Monitors hummed and beeped. The needles on various dials flipped back and forth like wiper blades. Crow waited for nausea, organ failure, decomposition, and death. Instead, he found himself ravenously hungry. (Why credit ravens with appetite? he wondered.) Whatever they brought, he ate and waited for more. Drecky and bland institutional foodstuffs, but beggars could not be choosers. Gradually his handlers recognized his increased capacity for consumption, and they began to cater to it. His feathers grew back, blacker than ever, with an incredible sheen. When they left in his cage an entire leg of lamb, garnished with champignons, Crow noticed he was growing.

His head soon bumped the top of the confinement facility. Scientists flocked (!) around him. They drew numerous blood samples, experimented with various menu options and vitamin combinations. He grew even more rapidly until his beak was the length of a research man's arm. Lucky for them, Crow was more interested than resentful. He was well taken care of for the first time in his life, and he thought to take advantage of it. He was willing to sacrifice a certain autonomy and freedom of movement in exchange for high-level catering. Up to a point, the point coming when they moved him to an airplane hangar.

By now, Crow was almost twenty feet tall, and he had experienced the gradual change in his point of view from ground level to something like normal elevation, except his feet, immense and horny, were still on the ground. His eyes had acquired a laser-like focus. He could count the buttons on a lab coat at two hundred yards. When he tried to hop, he left cracks in the concrete, and the scientists and press people who regularly gathered behind a mesh barrier inside the hangar fled in terror. "Don't worry," shouted one of the government's PR people, "this bird is no longer emitting Strontium 90, and the chains holding him are made of chromium steel." When had they applied the chains? How had he missed that? Were they slipping mickeys into his baked Alaska? He flapped his wings, and the wind nearly blew off the crowd's protective goggles.

He had become a freak, a monster, a scientific oddity, his image appearing everywhere on the History Channel, CNN, Fox. There were crows and crow handlers popping up all over the broadcast spectrum, on *Kelly Clarkson*, *Good Morning America*, and *Jimmy Kimmel Live!* On the internet, he was the most heavily trafficked meme, an emblem of comic disproportion and nuclear terror all at once. He was the brave new world that had been prophesied since Ray Bradbury wrote about kids growing giant mushrooms in their basements.

Crow was desperately alone. The sedge had withered from the lake, and no birds sang. Literally. He longed for conversation and was ecstatic when the briefly opened hangar doors allowed in a few flycatchers. But they hung back in the rafters, unable to believe he would not scarf them all up at once. Crow understood. He had to keep telling himself not to try to eat everything in sight.   All he could do was be folksy. "Howdy," he said. "I could use a little news. What's going on out there?"

"It really is true," one of them said. "It's really you. You're huge, I mean in every possible way."

"Well, I would look pretty big to you in any event." Then Crow began to tear up. "I don't want to grow anymore!" he croaked. He scooped up an entire side of beef in his beak and hurled it toward them. "Go ahead, you eat it!"

"Whoa, Crow, don't take it personally. We came to pay homage to the Big Bird, the one we all look up to, the living legend, proof that no matter what they throw at us, birds will not only survive, they will triumph." One of the flycatchers sidled up across the beam so he could whisper in Crow's giant ear. "But to be perfectly honest, we expected someone a little more confrontational, a little less accepting of the powers that be. I mean, Crow, it's cushy here, we get that, but you are the ultimate victim of government misconduct and environmental insult. Everyone needs to know where you stand. It's not like you have to go on a spree, like Rodan or Mothra."

The references were over Crow's head (not literally, of course), but he got the impression they were King Kong-like winged avatars, probably Japanese from the sound of it. He blew the annoying flycatchers out of the hangar with a single tidal wind wave of his wing. In Japan, Crow might have been a national hero on the order of Futubayama, the sumo wrestler. Here he was a sideshow, a victim who couldn't even cash in on his victimhood. But the flycatchers got him thinking beyond his own pain.

Entertainment? He would give them entertainment. He raised his beak and slammed it down on the chains of chromium steel. They shattered like glass. He strode forward and broke through the side of the hangar like something bad exploding out of a tin can. A crowd followed. Crow took several running steps, pumped his wings, and was airborne for the first time in months. He thought he would have to relearn everything about flying and the atrophy of his wings would send him crashing to the ground. But no! He had tremendous power. He could soar for miles, and altitude was no barrier. When he came down low over the suburbs, the roofs on the houses rippled and buckled. He let out a caw, and the trees shook. His gaze lit the streets on fire. Forget Rodan, he was Crowdan!

OK, he thought. Now let's get down to business.

He oriented himself and headed for Las Vegas.

Crow had seen a lot, not all of it pretty. He had looked upon the cold and unstunned sphere, as the poet says, and was still here, for better or worse, still ready to witness and participate. His own sense of being well worn made him dismissive of those birds who claimed to have seen it all. The worst was a tough-talking, foul-mothed grackle who hung out in Green-Wood Cemetery. The conversations tended to be monochromatic. "You see that, Crow, you see how those starlings book it as soon as the park uniforms roll up?" And "Them wild parrots, they think they're hot shit because they busted out of some cheap cage in the Bronx. But a couple a days later and no more three squares for free and they'll turn any trick for a bite to eat. Bird who looks as good as they do ought to have more self-respect." This diatribe was followed by conspiratorial racism that Crow couldn't abide: "You and me, Crow, if we was in charge, we'd send em all back where they come from. Mexico or Venezuela or El Salvador. You know what I'm saying."

Crow figured that the grackle picked up these attitudes from hanging around police stations, which the bird tended to do when not in the cemetery. Crow would have preferred never to have to listen to the bird, but he liked Green-Wood and kept coming back. It had the best trees in the city, from giant tulip trees to azalea bushes as big as a house. Besides, he was something of a connoisseur of burial grounds. The pools especially had a ceremonial formality, a profound emptiness that made him wish that the animal kingdom, or at least his branch of it, paid a little more attention to rituals of commemoration. On the other hand, fencing off a football field and filling it with stone markers didn't seem an effective way of negotiating with the spirits of the dead. What made anyone think they would keep to their side of the fence?

Crow tried to keep to himself in Green-Wood, sticking to some out-of-the-way spots, like Eucalyptus Path with its giant cedars of Lebanon, but one day he flew up the hill to the Samuel Morse monument to get a better view of Manhattan. The grackle made him as if Crow were under surveillance.

"Crow, I know you're an experience junkie, like you can't say no to a good story. I have been burning to tell you something you will not fucking believe." The grackle's whole modus vivendi seemed to be to try to impress Crow, to get a rise out of him. No wonder Crow had developed his blasé façade to the level of an art. So he thought. "Like I know some birds and we hang out at the Nineteenth in Manhattan. The cops there know us, and they toss a few things our way, just to keep themselves busy, you know, crime being down and all. So one of them mentions they busted a necrophiliac ring on the Upper East Side. It all went down in some fancy apartment near a funeral parlor."

Crow had no idea where this was going.

"So, have I got your attention? So, that gets us conversing, and one of our group says he knows someone, you know, *amici degli amici*, who is part of the same scene, behind a flower shop right near Sunset Park. Not far from here. How about that. You never know what's happening right under your own beak. But you don't have to be rich to be into this. You have to know some-body to be in on it, and I could get you in, Crow. Admit it, you're interested. I can tell. Bird like you is always looking to expand your range of metaphor, am I right?"

Not in this case, thought Crow. He knew something about violating the dead because it was more common than this grackle seemed to be aware. Lizards, whales, penguins, garter snakes, crows all had their—what to call them?—inanimate encounters, and Crow thought you could chalk it up to one cause: bad child rearing. These creatures had never learned the most basic lesson of being alive, which was to recognize when something else wasn't. If you couldn't figure that out, you would fail at the only thing—ostensibly—nature wanted you to do, which was make more of yourself. Crow was obviously no prude, but this was a not-very-interesting example of being as thick as two short planks. If these creatures were any stupider, they would have to be watered twice a week.

Nevertheless. Which is to say the vehemence of Crow's reaction was obviously some sort of defense mechanism. He couldn't stop thinking of an image of cold inertness. Nothing coming of nothing. All his erotic encounters tended to blend together, but they had one thing in common: backtalk. "Slow down Crow, what's the rush?" "A little more to the left, ahh." "Where did you learn how to do that? I don't like fancy." Etc. The same-sex thing was never a problem because everyone was usually cool and up front about their own desires. The "little death" was one thing, but having it on with someone who wasn't there and never coming back was something altogether different. Did Crow really need to see it or do it to understand it? He already knew that the desire for experience is a failure of imagination.

Nevertheless, Crow let the grackle know to let the friend of friends know he might drop around.

He found the flower shop, saw another crow who pretended nothing was up and ignored Crow's nod. Crow finally came out with it: "I'm looking for a one-way street."

"This is a club. Members only. Not some bullshit social-media Tinder hookup. Discretion and repeat visits are what the club is all about. Curiosity is discouraged. Think of this as an initiation." The bird waited to see if it sank in. "By the way, there's nothing more pathetic than an aging hipster with no cred. You might let the grackle know the next time you see him."

The crow led him to the roof of the flower shop, to what appeared to have once been a dovecot. It was covered with vines and near collapse, but you could get in and out, and prying eyes could not follow. The bird left Crow at the entrance. He dipped in.

Except for the rigid waxwing in the center, its legs stiff in the air, it was all quite decorous. Not a grackle, a raven, not even some deeply twisted warblers remarked on the thing in the center, as though it were furniture. Instead, they talked of the weather, public sculpture, various luxury destinations. Crow couldn't help noticing with some surprise that it was a bi-gendered group, more like a cigar bar than a locker room. Crow chose not to engage the discussion of roosting locations in Forte dei Marmi and the palm-tree blight in Portofino, and in the middle of that conversation without missing a beat, one of the birds hopped over and leapt on the corpse. After an instantaneous spasm, it hopped off. Other birds barely nodded or failed to register that they even noticed. But quickly, another took its place, and this time remained longer, clearly getting into it and the growing sense of being part of a theatrical performance. With each act, Crow felt his anonymity disappearing. How long before eyes turned to him in expectation? No spectators allowed except on the distaff side, but even there . . .

What did Crow do or decide not to do? Best leave that to the imagination of the reader, as an index of polymorphous perversity. It is more important to explore what Crow thought. That he never supposed depravity could be casual. He had always imagined it as a frenzy. That the abyss of another is exceeded only by the abyss of pure unknowing and unknowability. That this distance was nothing other than death itself. That, viewed from that distance, life—that is to say its physical processes—could be described as comically vile. That once you gave up the idea of a universal spirit, the enormity of coming into being and passing away—thrown into life and then at some point yanked or dragged out of it—could not really be justified. By what perverse calculus had such a principle come to dominate the universe? What did the birds think, that this club was an attempt to rescue a certain divinity for creaturehood by denying the true order of things? Really? That felt wrong on the face of it. Crow felt he was in danger of becoming a three-penny Socrates with principles.

Crow returned to the cemetery. He didn't care anymore what the grackle might have to say, and this time the bird actually avoided him. Crow could tell. Finally, their meeting became inevitable, but not without backup. A group of them confronted Crow near the grave of Leonard Bernstein.

"You are one loose cannon, Crow. That is the last time I hook you up. I heard all about it. You seriously weirded them all out, doing what you did. And you wouldn't stop. Like it was the lost Lenore come back to life. All that talk about taking off together, to Puerto Rico or Shangri-la or wherever, what was that about? As if she could answer. Don't tell me, I don't wanna know."

Crow refused to say. But he knew what he had done, and he knew what they had seen but not understood. He would not stop until he found a way to bring the dead back to life, so the sum of all being and nonbeing might be zero instead of always minus one. Did he have enough love within himself to revive the whole world? Or at least keep it going?

22. Crow and Invincible

(in memory of Stanislav Lem)

It happened in Flushing, referred to mistakenly as the second Chinatown, an ethnic designation Crow, wary of ghettoes, was loath to honor. Nevertheless, it was a neighborhood where much was diverting and tolerance for birds like him was relatively high. Of course, the markets attracted him, with their unusual fruits and vegetables that gave him the oddest sensations when he came in proximity. He dared not get too close because he sensed their hallucinogenic properties. A close second, however, were the restaurants. The skinned carcasses of ducks hanging in the windows were morbidly fascinating, occasions for schadenfreude. Only the starving would try to make a meal of him, and his own scrawny corpus trussed upside down would never be useful as culinary advertising. Tanks of black bass and tilapia seemed oblivious to confinement and fate. These places put it all on display.

The window of the Li Li on Union Street made a more profound impression. It was multi-tiered aquarium of sorts. There were crabs and lobsters, but in one section, the greenish water seemed to contain nothing but a sort of gray cloud. There was about it a latency, an inertness even, that signified a presence that had no state, something between living and dead. Something in the process of retreating into nonbeing. Crow, who was frequently and embarrassingly available, sensed his opposite. He swooped low and landed on a tower of empty cartons crowding the sidewalk.

He saw eyes. They did not look like things that saw. Or saw in a way that eyes didn't, with another sense of the visible. But they saw Crow, or so he sensed, because the thing in the tank suddenly lit up. Colors streamed across its rippled skin, and its tentacles curled and waved in the dank water. It had gone from utter passivity to a tentacular agitation. Its limbs unfurled up the sides of the tank in an exploration of escape. Crow stared at the hypnotic curlings and uncurlings, as the suckers opened and closed on the glass. Of course, thought Crow, the thing only seems not to see because it has no center, its mind is every-where, and its gaze leads back to nowhere. All of it thinks, all of it feels, and all of it knows. It has no self and so no unconscious, no shadow, no surprise. Its surface is the depth.

Crow felt a door opening somewhere in his head. He felt he could communicate with the thing even though there was no question of making sounds. But maybe there were sounds, good sounds and bad sounds in that world. There had to be. Just as there had to be good smells and bad smells, dark shades and light shades, gradations of every kind of stimuli. And this ugly centerless thing knew them and processed them all in the midst of an underwater world in which everything else was single-minded in its predatory pursuits.

Your up is our down, thought Crow through the open brain door. What are you?

My lack of definition bothers you (it thought). Nomencla-tural issues are not my interest, but I understand how catego-ry ambiguities can induce primal fear, even in crows, who are cynical about appearances. But you are wrong. I have a center. I have more than one. My limbs, which seem to fascinate you, don't necessarily even report to me. But I trust them to do what they need to do. It leaves me free for other things.

You command colors at will, Crow thought. I have only one color, which I can barely manage.

Bluish hues rippled across the rubbery, undulating shape. Crow got no message in return, only the sensation of being extraordinarily close to the world around him, as if he were wearing it all like a skin. Suddenly the octopus shot across the tank. Crow did not know how to describe the motion to himself. The tentacles closed like whips on nothing, on water, and yet it moved, as if it were propelled by its own idea.

Why is that so strange? (it thought). It's only a question of medium. How is it that you can elevate simply by moving your wings? That appears equally impossible.

Suddenly it did. Crow wondered how he could ever convince himself to fly again. But the thing in the tank radiated new colors, and Crow's mind was filled with distant but familiar thoughts. He remembered things he could not possibly have known, like sunlight filtered through a dozen feet of cold water in a tide pool, and the feeling of giant waves that register only as a slight rocking on the ocean floor. At the edge of a kelp forest, Crow tasted lobster for the first time. He was pursued by sharks, lost a tentacle down to a stump, found hiding places by instantaneous triangulation. The world was beautiful and menacing.

You plant thoughts, thought Crow.

Come closer was the response.

Crow felt his mind raided.

You read minds.

I mimic them. But I am incapable of judging.

How is it you can do these things?

I am like a grain of sand that through irritation becomes a pearl. I evolved. And unlike you, I probably have not reached a dead end. Parts of me remain potential. At least that's how it feels. I can grow new limbs.

You're in a tank. Confined. Ignored to a degree that has turned you gray.

There is no tank. That's what they think.

With that, the octopus began to sprout. Extraordinary objects grew out of its body: a pair of scissors, a monkey's paw, a set of gardening tools, a rubber tree, some Albert Ayler vinyl sides, an ersatz temple-style farmer's house from Hangzhou. The things erupted from the slick skin like bubbles, took form, then disappeared back into the creature's body, only to be replaced by something different and even more fantastic: a Fiat 1500, the collected works of Karl Ove Knausgaard, the Rosetta stone, a crow in Crow's very image. The hypnotic undulations, the sprouting and disappearing forms, the kaleidoscopic colors all made Crow believe he was dreaming. But his own dream state was only a feature of the octopus' imagining of everything that had ever passed through its sensory field. Which was, apparently, infinitely wide. The creature's amoebic shape was the sign of its liquid nature.

You don't mimic them all, you create them all, thought Crow, by your fluid will, your distributed synaptic configuration. How could I, a bird, have this insight unless it, too, was through you, made possible by you? You are the ocean of forms, and if you left off spawning shapes, where would I be? Where would anything be?

The octopus left the question hanging. But added the thought: In a cave, on an as-yet-undiscovered moon of the seventh planet, there is another just like me. A version of me, like many others. All versions without an original, all dispersed expressions of a single idea. Impossible to say if it was first, but on that moon, it imagined its own sea. It diverts itself by populating and repopulating the bare rock with whatever it imagines, whatever we together know. That is, everything. I would resist the temptation to call it/them/us God.

Suddenly hands reached into the tank and pulled the writhing creature out of the water. It went limp as a towel over a waiter's arm, wobbly as Jell-O. So, the octopus was not invincible after all.

Crow registered a final thought from that other alien source as it headed for the kitchen: Don't worry. I only appear to be doomed. But it's all of you who are subject to change. I'm here, I was here, I will be here again. But in a year or even less, everything you see around you will be different. This restaurant will have a new name. Half the wait staff will be working in Sunset Park. Popularity will wane. Other cartons will replace the ones you are sitting on. I'll still be in this same tank, but no one you see on the street will be the same. No one on any planet in any solar system in the universe. Even you, Crow. Especially you.

Crow watched the watchers. No one watched Crow. Everywhere he went he saw them with their telephoto prostheses, their vision magnified to the point of identifying tail feathers and even eye color at vast distances. But he himself was invisible and considered this anonymity nature's gift. No one paid him any attention, assuming that all the birds that looked like him were the same. When it comes to crows, seen one, seen them all. A million lives a dozen stories. Or less. Or fewer.

The jabiru storks, golden crested cranes, and flightless kagus drew the watchers like magnets. Crow followed a pair of bird hunters through the cloud forest of Costa Rica, not far from San José. They were leading a gaggle of Spanish hospitality representatives on a quest to view the resplendent quetzal. Through the thick fog the two bird hunters mimicked the call of the male. All around them the birds answered back but stayed out of sight, as obscure as the voice of a deity. Crow had to admit the quetzals were a sight. But more than that he appreciated the game they were playing, leading the humans along until their necks bent under the weight of 1000-millimeter telephoto cannons and fishing vests jammed with phones, bird books, maps, chargers, granola bars, notebooks, and extra lenses.

They had come at the wrong time, at the beginning of the rainy season, because their package tour had booked it. The resplendent quetzal would be their nemesis bird, the species they would pursue for all time until they ran it to ground (with help, of course). Their lives were sure to become nothing more than a record of tactical encounters, and as for their conversations, Crow had overheard them all too often: "I was hiding in a tree blind in the Algarve when suddenly . . ." and "It was on Mount Kilimanjaro that I first saw . . ." and "If you really want to see a Bird of Paradise, then you have to visit a bird paradise. The place to go is Papua New Guinea." Crow, who had been almost everywhere, had never been to New Guinea, either half, but even among crows it had legendary status. Was that on Crow's bucket list? Did Crow even have a bucket list?

Crow often wondered if it was a case of becoming what you behold. Birds flocked, and, sure enough, so did birders. They looked alike. Crow recalled being in the Everglades, in June, when it was already a steaming jungle, and found himself at the edge of Mrazek Pond. There on the far shore was a literal herd, a gaggle, a pack of birdwatchers. Their clothes, hats, and sun visors were rumpled, as if the birders had spent time jammed into an overnight bag, and their tripods made them seem as if they were a team of surveyors, come to mark out the next Disney World. There were so many of them that there were no birds to be seen. Crow thought for minute that if he stuck around, they might make him into a nemesis bird. Instead, their camera motor drives remained silent as Crow retained his invisibility. He struck off along the Gumbo Limbo trail to listen to the migratory songbirds.

Crow's favorite birdwatcher was a kid in Myanmar who had been press ganged into service as a guide near Inle Lake. No sense trying to explain how Crow wound up there, during a brief window when fighting had died down and you could visit the floating temples. The guide's main job was leading unsuspecting visitors on a grueling forced march through mountain tea plantations to jungle temples, but in the course of his work he had developed his own app-like invention, a scheme for accessing all the bird calls he had collected on his phone. It wasn't really all that useful or necessary since the kid had memorized all the calls anyway and could reproduce most of them by imitation. But the phone thing seemed to impress the tourists more than his mimicry, and it kept their minds off the killing pace of their hike. Crow hung around and made some noise just to see if he could get a rise out of the ranger, his voice on tape so to speak. The kid shook his head and kept moving.

Exotic Burma! But birds need not be special, like a male Congo peafowl, or endangered, like the Maui parrotbill, to be a nemesis, just unseen by you. Crow knew there were kin of his that were endangered, the island crows of Rota, for example, but somehow that seemed like a technicality, sort of like saying that English speakers in Borneo were endangered. There were plenty of English speakers around, probably too many. Rare birds are obvious, but others can haunt, as Crow well knew, and they don't have to be good looking. They can be downright ugly. And that may be why Crow was bothered and bewildered by the shoebill.

How was Crow even aware of the shoebill? There were certain birds you just knew about—by reputation or rumor or legend or jokes ("Why did the chicken cross the road?"). Crows talked about the shoebill because it was uglier than they reputedly were, a bird you could defensively demean. But still, for whatever reason, people wanted to see it, and would travel thousands of miles to do so. Why? Crow, the invisible, imagined its hideous and comic aspect in his dreams. He conjured everything that was the opposite of himself, of his good qualities, that is, something gross, garish, and beakishly distorted, worse than a pelican. But these were only fantasies, and Crow was determined to find out why this thing had status in the human world (and Crow, as well as crows, had none).

The only way to understand a mania is to share it, and that starts with going wherever and doing whatever the obsession commands. The shoebills he had heard about lived near Entebbe, across the water at the edge of Lake Victoria. Like a lost tribe, like the Jews of Mbale. So, Crow sucked it up, put up with the privations of global travel, and went in search. Hanging out at the ranger station, where the staff was as heavily armed as ivory poachers, it didn't take Crow long to identify a group of humans that were even dottier than he was. Crow saw them approach the station from the water, their car strapped to nothing more than a floating piece of wood. Crow had seen birds take some pretty strange ferries, on the backs of hippos, crocs, and even rhinos, but this exemplified the triumph of a belief in self-levitation. Two of the rangers ambled out to the shore to tie up the precarious float, but before they arrived, the battered rental Land Rover rolled off the raft and onto terra firma. It was a family from Brooklyn. A stray complaint about loading the freezer at the food co-op gave them away. Come to think of it, this group looked vaguely familiar. Crow might well have spent time in their garden, watching various felines battle each other for territorial supremacy. Why did anyone think cats were cute?

The guide boat to which everyone transferred was a wooden dory with a tiny outboard that looked like it had been stolen from Cape Cod after a nor'easter. The tour guide, a titanically tall woman in fatigues and a sidearm, addressed them all like a military gathering. "Alright! Listen here. You're just in time. One more minute and you would have no chance of seeing the shoebill. But, as of now, your chance is eighty percent." The group looked at each other with relief. "You will get in the boat now."

They set out into the steamy papyrus marsh. This sea of grass was spotted by spongy hummocks where the fisherman wove their huts. These human beings seemed to Crow just another larger version of cormorant birds. They watched the tourist birders with stoic indifference. They pointed no cameras back at the cameras pointing at them. What on earth did they make of these *mzungus* wandering through their world of sun and water? Perhaps they thought of them as illusions, phantoms. Wasn't Crow also a *mzungu* of sorts, a creature who wandered around? Albeit not a white one. The boat worked its way through a labyrinth of channels, while their guide sat stolidly in the bow, never lifting her binoculars and keeping one hand on the butt of her pistol. Shoebills, Crow imagined, were imposing but elusive, confined to some routine or other. In truth, they were elusive because they hardly moved.

As the boat glided through the shallow water, the guide announced, "Our chances of seeing the shoebill are at least fifty percent." She had changed her tune. This announcement was greeted with disconcerted muttering. Crow searched among the reeds. He had to adjust his eyes to the grayness of the birds, get in tune with their glacial pace. He circled low overhead. He saw one, perched impassively on a low rise just above the papyrus. It was the ugliest thing Crow had ever seen, an exaggeration of a bird, all gimlet stare and gullet. Its beak looked as if it had been tied on, like a goofy Halloween mask except for the nasty hook at the end. So, this was it. No one else saw the creature, not even the guide, and it seemed to have no desire to be seen.

Just then the guide looked at her watch and announced, "Our chance of seeing the bird is now zero percent. It does not like to come out in the afternoon. All its feeding is done by early morning. We will go back."

"We should have checked the bird's habits before we came. That's what parents are for," said one of the younger members of the group. "If we don't make it back on that ferry, we will have died in vain."

One of the parents tried to be upbeat. "We can still imagine the bird, and isn't that better than seeing the thing and going, 'Really?'"

"Really? We already missed the gorillas because you said they were too touristy, and now this," came the response.

The guide looked at the upstart and said, "We do not make promises. The animals do as they please. It is a good lesson to learn."

"Maybe twenty percent good, or ten," muttered the tyke.

The boat made a sharp turn almost in front of the shoebill and headed back through the marsh.

Nemesis bird indeed. Crow landed near the shoebill and watched the boat disappear out of the marsh. He thought he detected a snicker from the bird. Probably the human was right about preferring fantasy to reality, or seventy percent right, at least. Why was Crow even here? What had he expected or hoped for?

That was what the shoebill asked him: "What are you doing here? You ought to get yourself to higher ground."

Crow thought, Man, this bird really is funky looking. He said, "I heard you are old. I heard you come from Egypt. I heard you've been around before paper, before writing, before media generally, and before the pharaohs and the pyramids."

"Before empires, kings, enslavement, the parting of the sea," the bird added, all the time concentrating intently on the water. "You probably can't imagine why anyone would come looking for me. I confess, I myself am a little puzzled." The bird seemed to be waiting for something. "But you never answered my question: why are you here?"

Crow didn't need to think. "Because I wanted to know what it's like to be looked at, to be pursued, to be seen."

As ugly and stolid as it was, the shoebill made an incredibly fast dart into the water and came up with a small fish in its beak. The fish was gone in seconds. Definitely not how Crow dealt with his gustatory impulses.

"I look for no one and see only what I need and want to see," said the shoebill between gullet gulps. "But Crow, you know very well what it's like to have a nemesis bird, to be always in pursuit of an unseen, invisible being, whose hue and outline haunt your waking mind. You've come as far as a marsh in Uganda when you already know the bird intimately, its diet, habitat, range, behaviors, even its phobias and eccentricities. You know your nemesis bird, Crow, you've even seen it, and it isn't me. But after all this time, you don't quite believe it's real, do you?"

Crow caught a glimpse of his reflection in the murky water of Lake Victoria. He stared at it for some time. "No," he answered, "I don't."

24. Crow Travels Extensively and Concludes that He and the Globe Are a Mile Wide and an Inch Deep

As should be evident by now, Crow was not immune to the blandishments of the travel and leisure industry. *Deracinated* was the word he sometimes heard. That was harsh, Crow thought, as he perched on the top of a bus traveling along the Avenue Simon Bolivar near the Parc des Buttes-Chaumont. He took wing, as they say, up the passageway to Jardin Bergeyre, from where he could see all the way to Montmartre, turning pink in the setting sun. It was beginning to grow dark along Karl Johansgatan, and the winter streetlights were already on in the park. Crow felt the chill, but the lights and the hubbub inside the Grand Café cheered him up. Oslo was a place to feel like a stranger and enjoy it, outside looking in, like Bruges, Hanoi, or Bogota. Who would think of living there? Crow saw a mime in the park, surrounded by only a handful of people beginning to stamp their feet against the cold. The mime seemed to be performing an elaborate routine about escaping from a narrow-walled room that was slowly closing in. Everyone in the sparse crowd spoke Spanish, but with different accents.

A sudden sound got Crow's attention. People were in the streets in the fancy neighborhood near Recoleta Cemetery—even there—banging on pots and pans. It was obvious why: another power outage in the middle of the hottest summer on record in Buenos Aires. Crow had to get some shade, so he hunkered down in the shadow of a gigantic movie screen that had been set up in the plaza near the Teatro Colón. At this stage of the game, Crow couldn't ignore the fact that he gravitated to large public buildings, the more ceremonial the better. He tended to meet a certain class of bird there.

People had gathered to watch a tribute to David Bowie, all his videos, one after another, Ziggy, Major Tom, Serious Moonlight. Clips from the films washed over them, *Merry Christmas, Mr. Lawrence*, *The Man Who Fell to Earth*, *The Hunger*. Crow had a theory about vampires, that they were put on earth to teach the living, especially medical professionals and hedge-fund managers, about the dangers of perpetual existence. Now was forever, and forever was always now, until it wasn't. But Crow could get his head around it. If you come from a city, he thought, you should always have another city buried in your psyche, a shadow city, an alternative grid, another set of moods and temperatures. A Buenos Aires of the mind.

Crow followed the bicyclists along the dusty tracks that threaded among the temples on the plain of Bagan. He could see the Irrawaddy River in the distance, running low and murky. The decrepit tour launches with their faded blue, green, and white paint, lay moored and empty. Crow turned back to the temples, some gleaming white, others dirty brown, the color of earth. An earthquake? a tornado? genocidal war? had lopped off many of their delicate metal crests, like flowers cut after their blossoms faded. Some looked like stubby fingers with broken knuckles. They spread across the plain in a stone orgy of devotion and self-promotion, as far as the eye could see (which, in Crow's case, was not that far, but he got the idea). In an alcove, he watched a boy paint a meticulous and automatic copy of a nearly vanished temple fresco.

He followed the cyclists along the canals of Amsterdam, watching as they nearly knocked down a dozen tourists who didn't know the rules of the narrow cobblestoned streets. Amsterdam had the busiest sky Crow had ever seen, and for all the water everywhere, Crow felt strangely hemmed in. People seemed to be drunk and pissing everywhere he went. Or perhaps that was Brussels.

The imperial capitals of Europe—Crow had a fondness for them as he got older, for their symmetries, public poise, and aesthetic irrelevance. On the worn paving stones of the beautiful post-quake Baixa in Lisbon he felt like promenading in a penguin's garb. In Turin, he skulked among the colonnades and kept out of the sun. In Madrid, he pecked grapes in Retiro Park and felt justified. In Milan, he perched on the cathedral and looked down on the galleria.

From such an altitude, it seemed to Crow that the Yucatan was the greatest pyramid scheme ever invented. Calakmul rose up from the flat forest like a hand trying to claw its way out of the strangling vegetation. From the peak of the pyramid, Crow could imagine the entire peninsula, the entire Mayan world, as if he were seeing it in front of him: the flamingos of Celestún—victims of their own dietary proclivities, but they wore it well—the long canoes on the Usumacinta River, the potholed road in Sian Ka'an and the constant sound of surf, the Lacandon souvenir sellers at Bonampak, dressed in white cloth, more like birds than humans. Crow was sure they were related to him, that he could understand their language, their belief that the *blancos* were phantoms that left trash and money in their wake.

Crow followed the money. His favorite Brooklyn perch was his favorite bank, in Williamsburg, but now a giant sneaker store with racks of cheap clothing under its dome. Money changes everything, and it travels faster that you can, Crow. The notions shops, butchers, and pharmacies were all restaurants. But they kept the old signs and the floor tiles inside for retro authenticity, perfect for Brooklyn arrivistes, who would rather be, if they could have afforded it, you know where.

The banks were all transitioning away from money, fragmenting like shrapnel into a thousand pop-up service centers, filled with youngish customer service representatives and no paper anywhere. The last great tower of legal tender, that Alhambran beacon, stood empty, its clockface blank, waiting for the developers. In the interim: a flea market. It was inevitable, and, after all, not so bad. The world of Crow's itinerant mind resembled nothing so much as a flea market, *un mercado de pulgas*, *les puces*, expanding exponentially from Lagos and the Old Biscuit Mill in Cape Town to Unter den linden and the Tiergarten. San Telmo, the Parque Lezama, Usaquen, Porta Portese, the Rose Bowl, Togo Shrine, Saint-Ouen. Crow never looked for bargains, only the breadth of selection, variety, shades of color, and the glint of light on metal, plastic, and gems. Too much furniture at Brimfield for his taste. He admired; he didn't consume. He was jaded to all but the most exquisite of sensations. (Not true! Crow was getting literary again.) He saw much to covet and nothing to possess. The smell of an antique hand coffee grinder on a blanket in Palma de Mallorca sent his head reeling.

He moved on, as the whole world threatened to tie him down. In the back of a pickup truck near Las Cruces, New Mexico, crowded by shotguns and a gas can, a hippie vagabond was busy tearing the pages out of a bulging address book and letting each one catch the wind like a leaf. "It's my book of expectations," he said, and added, "maybe we'll meet down the road." Crow followed the twisting, fluttering paths of the pages as the wind carried them across the fly-swarming Rio Grande, or north, as far as the eye could see. Halfway up the continent, he could sense the opening before he saw it, into the immensity of James Bay. I've come too far, he thought. Time to sell the canoe. In reality, Crow was only looking for a perch. But the branches were too crowded in Terre Haute, crowded with blackbirds on their way god knows where, shitting a white tide on everything. And overpasses in Austin and Tucson were no place to shelter because the bats were on their own mad itinerary, probably toward Mexico and caves in the Sonoran Desert. In Halong Bay, Crow could play the tourist, put on the pineapple-print shirt and take a rickshaw, like the old days, when he fantasized about buying a Leica and a motorbike and heading off into the bush, ten clicks down the road where Charlie was laying down some heavy shit and the people needed to see the truth about the war. Crow would tell it all in his photographs.

Rome was a nest of feral cats. Best not to linger, in spite of the interrupted garbage pickups. On the island of Houat, Crow followed an old man carrying a flower behind his back as if it were a gift he was hiding for a sweetheart. Along the coast of Zanzibar, the sound of the surf was as rhythmic and gentle as the bending of women gathering fishing nets. Ciudad del Este in Paraguay: Shopping China, Shopping Yangs, Jebai Center, the dream of a common language from capitalist detritus, whole families trooping back and forth across the Friendship Bridge between Brazil and Paraguay, or was it Argentina? Crow was confused. Was it two rivers or three? The walked and drove laden with bags of toilet paper, blood pressure cuffs, plastic thermoses, weapons. The Parana River below was littered with small boats. Crow watched the traffic from a cliff like a bribed customs agent while money changed hands.

Itineraries of dust and frontiers. Every departure had become a little death. It seemed unnatural to sit still, but Crow forced himself. He felt he had come to the end of the line, some line. He was all the places he had ever been and, almost equally, all the places he had never been but knew as mysterious names. Images streaked with color flashed through his mind. Were they birds he barely remembered or ones he imagined he would one day see? Where was Crow headed, after all?

"I'm a wanderer," said Crow to himself, "a kind of hobo, without family or friends. Where another bird's life might begin, that's exactly where mine ends." Crow watched the traffic back and forth on the international bridge. How to stop? Where to stop? When to stop?

Crow had the sudden notion that by sitting there he might perfect a technique. Waiting would engender the accrual of substance, and substance was what he lacked. If he could conserve to the point of stasis, he might approach absolute zero in terms of energy committed, emotion invested, nostalgia enabled. He might theoretically live forever, in which case everything sooner or later would pass before his eyes. He would see without looking, understand without repeating himself in a thousand different places.

But he couldn't sit still. "I feel myself to be a blur," said Crow to no one.

Crow will never stop because what he is after he already has and is constitutionally incapable of realizing. It's all around him wherever he is and is always seemingly out of reach: one hundred percent of the world as it is.

25. Crow's Nest
(for H. Owsley)

It had often been remarked, by friends and enemies alike, that Crow needed a clutter consultant. Had he been able to watch it, YouTube might have helped a lot. The great benefit of this platform is not that you can follow its instructions but rather that every conceivable problem has been faced—more than once. The problem of home organization, for example. You are not alone in having too much stuff. You are not even you (that is, someone with a unique experience). Some comfort in that, Crow supposed. Things inside Crow's nest had reached such a pass that there were only two regrettable but nevertheless distinct alternatives: divest or move. The issue wasn't so much a lack of space but a depressing sense of accumulating chaos. Faced with unpalatable choices, Crow did what he always did: nothing. That is, he waited for a sign to move him. He hoped that would come from examining what was all around him.

Beginning with: a scrap of narrow purple ribbon from a church in Bahia that said *Lembrança do Nosso Senhor do Bomfim.* A plastic packet of soy sauce from Beverly Soon's Tofu Restaurant and a paper fortune from a fortune cookie from the same establishment prophesying, "The more you change, the more you become yourself." This Crow pinned up over the entrance to the nest and repeated as a mantra.

A yellow silk tassel and a tiny brass bird from the headdress of the Saiō-Dai when she endeavored to empty herself of her ego in purification rituals at the Kamigamo and Mie shrines. Half a page from the *Genji Monogatari* with a small illustration of

Prince Genji of the Lightning (*Hikari Genji*) traveling through remote mountains. A McDonald's Happy Meal toy Ninja Turtle. Crow was skeptical of animal avatars in technologically advanced societies, but though he didn't believe in God, he hoarded certain "lucky" objects. Green, pink, and yellow plastic grass from Easter baskets. The world is a colorful place, after all!

Crow pilfered a bullet, .45 caliber Smith and Wesson, from Lalo Salamanca. It happened in Juárez. And here Crow had to face, yet again, the fact that his crib, his nest, his man-cave was not merely the artifact of acquisitive habits, not simply a graveyard of enthusiasms or a mental travelogue but an incriminating brief, a grand jury-level indictment: Crow was a thief. He stole. All his world traveling was mere pretext for expanding his hoard, and every city was a strategic challenge. Fine gold threads and a piece of ermine-topped red velvet from one of the Queen's robes. A holy card with St. George slaying a dragon. "Pray for us, St. George!" it entreated. A dog tag with "Frieda" inscribed on it. An ancient bulb from a 1938 epinephrine atomizer. A small child's beaded leather moccasin that said on the bottom, "Stop and climb—it's still a dime!" A blue pom-pom tassel from a girl's bedspread. (Crow regretted that theft, a needless one, even more arbitrary than St. Augustine's theft of a peach.) An old brass French horn key. A blue glass marble. A page of a program from a Youth for Understanding concert in Buenos Aires in 1971, including Sibelius' "Onward, Ye Peoples!" and Palestrina's "Lux Eterna."

A two-dollar bill. A scrap from the Hidden Pictures page of a *Highlights* magazine, spied from the transom of a children's dentistry waiting room and torn out and stolen in just one swoop.

But more impressive was a single daring daylight raid that netted: an origami crane of gold, a gold zodiac charm bracelet, a gold pinky ring with a tiny bow and diamond, and a brooch with two doves drinking from a fountain etched and then painted to imitate lapis lazuli. How did Crow manage to pull it off? By casing the place and waiting until vacation emptied the house? Hardly. Crow had seen and heard enough about noir to know that hitmen got away with the most atrocious acts by striking in front of everyone. Horror and fear would prevent witnesses from recalling what they had seen, much less intervening. "I . . . I . . . I really don't know what the bird looked like, officer. All I know is it was enormous, as big as a condor, even bigger." A paper umbrella from a Samoan Fog Cutter at Trader Vic's. A flyer in French from Arnaud's restaurant, or maybe it was Antoine's—Crow's memories of New Orleans tended to run together like the notes in a Dixieland clarinet solo. An aqua-colored golf visor from a Michigan City, Indiana golf course, signed by Arnold Palmer, "To Helen with love, keep it in the fairway, Arnie."

A Bernie Sanders campaign button. Nothing special here except as a symbol of Vermont's intimate political culture. Crow plucked it off the lapel of Howard Dean's down jacket as he left his dry cleaner in Burlington. No security detail was visible. A soft pink plastic flower stolen right off a girl's swim cap at the Tonawanda Swim Club when she turned to look south at the approaching funnel cloud as it touched down and the lifeguard blew his whistle and screamed, "Everyone out of the pool and into the clubhouse NOW!" A pack of L & M cigarettes stolen off the seat of an aqua 1969 Chevy Nova with a three-speed manual transmission. An autographed picture of the Cisco Kid from 1958. A white evening glove, full length, a tiny denim head scarf, and a red high heel taken from Barbie and Tammy doll cases on a front porch somewhere in Colorado. Two acrylic fingernails with swallows painted on them.

A length of tape from a Joni Mitchell cassette, or maybe it was a Phoebe Snow cassette, Crow couldn't remember because he liked them both equally. A roach clip with feathers. No need to worry about keeping it concealed since it was all legal now. A Boone's Farm screw cap. A desiccated clove of garlic to keep vampires away. Here again, Crow, skeptical of legends, wives' tales, and superstitions, nevertheless considered it foolish not to take advantage of an easily available potential prophylactic. Proof positive: He had never been bitten by one.

A Duane Reade receipt that was long enough because of the useless information about promotions it contained to be wound around the inside of his nest several times, like swaddling. An eagle's feather and a piece of dried sage from an offering on a Lakota reservation. (At least this is what Crow told anyone who visited. In fact, he swapped a small plastic football with green and white ribbon streamers from the MSU stadium for it. The eagle who traded him the feather hesitated, saying, "And I'm supposed to do what with this, exactly? But I kind of like the color scheme, and I love the fight song you were humming just now.") Remnants of a crawfish tail from Alabama. In the same vein, a tiny chicken bone from a Voodoo offering left in a park in New Orleans. A Pabst Blue Ribbon label. A Clark's Teaberry gum wrapper. A Squirrel Chew wrapper. The Teaberry wrapper to remind him that some things are simply inedible; the Squirrel Chew to remind him that some things are impossible to get enough of.

A yellowing plastic eye, crafted for the Halloween trade, but he told everyone he had plucked it from Tucker Carlson. Crow kept it in his nest as a caution against hubris. "Why," his friends asked earnestly, "would you peck out human eyes on national television?" Crow was upfront: "I should just sit there on a bust like a *meshuganah* raven and do nothing but croak 'Nevermore'?"

More recently, Crow was suspected of stealing a paper boarding pass—possibly the last one ever issued—from a passenger arriving at JFK from LAX.

Seeing them all gathered here in his place, he understood they were not arbitrary and the events they connected were not random. Instead of cleaning out the clutter, he realized that it was already perfectly organized on the only level that mattered. He sat and waited for the full picture to emerge.

At night all cats are gray. And all crows are black. Black as coal, black as the sun eclipsed from the sky. This dream of invisibility obsessed Crow and prompted him to make a study of deception.

It was everywhere in the animal and vegetable worlds, and the perfect paradox, the root condition of existence. On the one hand, you needed to make yourself *known* to the right members of your kind in order to keep things going. You had to stand out, display that plumage, do that weird dance, or kick some ass with a set of horns, show your teeth (assuming you had some) in order to guarantee attention and attraction. Crow was pretty sure even amoebas lit up or turned green, though he hadn't ever seen an amoeba. Amazingly, Crow was pretty successful in that regard. It wasn't like he had any extra outfits to put on. Only basic black, but always in good taste and never out of style. Although it is true that upon his arrival among a group of Andean cock-of-the-rocks recently escaped from the Bronx Zoo, one of them remarked, "So, the undertakers from Brooks Brothers are here." Nobody ever said that to ravens. They had that polish, that sharkskin sheen. All runway, all the time.

But it's not what you wear, it's how you wear it. And Crow looked and felt fresh in his own feathers. He didn't need disguises or surprises. On the other hand, there was the constant pressure to master invisibility, the dark art of clouding others' vision. Conveying disinformation, exploiting assumptions, propagating beliefs, encouraging the use of the subjunctive in if clauses contrary to fact. For two reasons. The first was to avoid confrontations that could be hazardous to your health. He knew of macaws that came on as dull as dishwater, blah gray. Of course, it made sense, especially in light of illegal trafficking. Not something Crow had to worry about, at least not yet. But was it worth it? He had heard there were fish that looked just like rocks, couldn't tell them apart except for the occasional air bubble. And some insects looked like sticks, stones, or leaves. Frogs and lizards wouldn't even know they were there, even though they were hard-wired to eat everything that wasn't nailed down. To have to go around constantly in some stupid getup just to keep the preds off your back, who could put up with it? At some point you would have to say, I really need to have at least one good look, just one outfit so that somewhere someone would do a double take at my appearance and say *"terrible!"* in a French accent. Crow had even less good to say about the reptiles and others who copied the style of more dangerous competitors, like coral snakes. He had seen a butterfly that could imitate five other kinds of butterflies that tasted really nasty. Wannabees looking for cover. If you can't stand the heat, get out of the kitchen was Crow's attitude. He had a certain amount of respect for shrimp with big claws. They were ready to menace even before the clippers actually worked. Crow figured the bluff came off about sixty percent of the time. Not bad odds for a shrimp.

The other side of that coin was more aggressive: the hunt by any means necessary. The fish that looked like a rock wasn't just hiding out, it was waiting for dinner to come along, maybe one of those shrimp. The more you thought about it, the heavier things got. Take fireflies. Crow liked them. They provided diversion of a summer evening, a relief from the monotony of darkness. But some types of females were bad news, just "venom wearin denim" as the song goes, able to light up in all kinds of inappropriate ways just to get guys hot and turn them into dinner. Worse than spiders: no chance even to get off. Crow once heard a survivor complain, "Eat, eat, eat! Doesn't anybody want to fuck anymore?"

Happily, Crow was more or less out of that Darwinian loop. He took whatever was on offer, and he always came as he was. He didn't have a lot of enemies, and he never had to go to the extreme of playing dead, like chickens or pigeons do. There may have been one exception, but that was more a matter of disbelief than outright thanatosis. Despite his sang-froid, however, he found himself increasingly fascinated by the notion of becoming something else, someone else, donning a completely new identity.

The idea didn't come from the hallucinogenic shit the Yucatan jay in the Bronx had laid on him. Crow was visiting some diminutive cousins in Michigan. He was sitting on a clothesline with a bunch of starlings taunting a bulldog named Danger. Out in the field in the back, he noticed a group of kids who looked from a distance like they had a skin disease. On closer aerial examination, he discovered that it wasn't their skin but the clothes they wore. Their mottled green and brown outfits seemed to be based on a coloring-book idea of what a forest looked like, or what it looked like to a creature who actually lived there, like a bear or a deer.

Camo. That was a form of bad news Crow understood very well. So-called sportsmen in desert camo. Forest camo. Three color, five color, Arctic Yeti, or something that looked like Swamp Thing, covered with fake Spanish moss. Crow watched the kids wander through a field with their plastic AR-15s, except they weren't plastic, that is, they weren't toys. One of the tykes opened up on a dead birch tree and quickly chopped it in half. There wasn't an animal in sight. Crow wondered why they needed the gear, since big guns made up for certain evolutionary disadvantages, like standing out like a sore thumb and not being able to smell anything or hear high-pitched sounds or see without glasses. You just stand there looking cute, and when something moves, you shoot. These kids were looking at him. Crow beat it out of there.

There weren't any stuffed heads in Crow's trophy room, but he couldn't get rid of the image of the kids in camo, creatures from another planet, super predators. He longed for predatory invisibility, but how to get it? He couldn't order from a catalogue or cover himself with leaves or imitate a houseplant. Wearing fur, aside from its political implications, was impossible and wouldn't fool anyone. Or would it?

And then it came to him: Confusion might be worth more than concealment. You might hide in plain sight by making it impossible for any creature to comprehend what you were. The secret of disidentification. Animal? Vegetable? Mineral? Neither this nor that, nothing that they know, hence nothing at all. Ambiguous as a pair of culottes or a kilt. Instinct would be confounded—at least for the short term. In certain circumstances, even an instant's hesitation could be a huge advantage, enough to give Crow "three steps toward the door," as the song goes.

Crow was what he was, but only apparently. Crow knew he

was more than his appearance betrayed, bland as Clark Kent and common as a pair of loafers. He had always suspected there was another half of him, sensed but unknown even to himself. Could that part be made manifest to sew bewilderment and cloud minds with indecision? Could he summon it into visibility when needed by sheer force of will? Part Crow, part Siberian huskie, with one blazing blue eye? Part Crow, part T-Rex, his vestigial inheritance? A collage Crow, a were-Crow.

At that moment, Crow was circling Harlem, a neighborhood he liked to visit because he stood out less. Despite low-level Russian financiers putting up apartments and the obvious gentrification of the streetscape, this was still a place for people of color—Crow's color. He spotted a group on a corner near the Abyssinian Baptist Church. (Where else? Crow knew a cultural icon when he saw one.) They were dressed for services and maintained the formality of an earlier time. Hats all around— broad-brimmed fedoras and a veiled pillbox with topaz decorations. A minority within a minority, Crow thought. He landed and very carefully sidled up and among them. They didn't seem to pay much attention, and he was there for a time, just listening to their speech, polite and familiar, until one of them addressed him: "Good morning, Mister Bird, what brings you to our community on the Sabbath?" Another said, "Perhaps it is hungry or thirsty. These birds feast on what others scorn, but little is left to waste here, and it must seem a desert much like the Sinai." A third one, in her veiled pillbox, added, "Then we should not ask, we should give."

Whereupon she reached into the jacket pocket of her vintage '60s Chanel houndstooth suit, took out a handkerchief, and unwrapped a crust of something saved from the morning fellowship get-together, a biscuit it looked like. She put it down on the curb. Crow sampled, politely. He thought about the impulse of generosity, how unprecedented it was, how it was the most spontaneous, even natural, of occurrences in the real world and yet the most surprising and mysterious. Don't ask, give. The admonition gave Crow an inkling of what must happen in order for him to set himself apart from all like him, to become something different. It was a small thing but better than camo, the ultimate disguise of becoming whatever you chose to be, perhaps something better. Crow transfigured. Yet it was impossible unless he could achieve a gymnastic feat that his body had not been designed for. He imagined his whole being as malleable and expressive, like 3D printing from rewritten software. Like clay in the hands of a divine sculptor, on the sixth day of creation before everything had been named.

Crow looked at the crumbs and smiled. Birds cannot smile or frown or laugh or cry. Crow was perfectly aware of this. But he smiled as if he had no beak, smiled as a child might have drawn his visage, preposterous and radiant. A Pentecostal smile.

The woman with the biscuit pointed this out to her friends as joyful news on the Sabbath, a sign and a wonder. Then she addressed Crow directly: "I can see the spirit moves you. But Mr. Bird, it's not so easy as that. The leopard has never lost its spots nor the tiger its stripes, and not for want of trying. Consult the Bible, the book for everything that lives. Only by passing through the eye of a needle, like the camel, will you finally stand before the gates of paradise. Which is where you belong and will at last be seen for what you really are."

27. Qrow

There were things Crow knew. There were things Crow knew he didn't know. And there were things Crow knew but didn't know he knew. But what worried him were the things he didn't know he didn't know. The known knowns. The known unknowns. The unknown knowns. But above all, the unknown unknowns. The intimation of them shadowed his days and clouded his thinking. How many times had he experienced the truism that discovery only increased his sense of ignorance? Voids of data, information, knowledge had to be everywhere but all imperceptible, and it was too late to pretend they didn't exist.

On the other hand, what if he, Crow, were to discover something heretofore truly unknowable and suddenly to know he knew it? It might be lurking in the most trivial or arbitrary-seeming connection between, say, a poinsettia deposited in the trash post-Christmas and the dark red of a passing late-model used car. The thought, perception, hint, whatever, would set in motion a train of associations that couldn't be stopped until it was careening down the track of obsession. Or maybe it was like a rack of pool balls struck by the cue ball. The triangle exploded, sending monads bouncing off each other and the side rails, only to come to rest in the form of a new pattern. Each stroke would require new thinking, new planning. New suspicions. New allegiances. New friends.

Crow reflected fondly on a time before the discovery of black holes, massive and invisible. How simple the universe must have seemed, big as it was. But at least they had been predicted. They even gave evidence of their vast negativity. They perturbed the nothingness of space. Dark matter, on the other hand—where had the idea come from? In what agitated dream was it born? By definition unknowable: colorless, odorless, tasteless, pure concept but somehow necessary to prop up the whole epistemological system and keep it from collapsing on itself in a giant vacuumed whoosh.

In this condition of doubt, suspicion, and vulnerability, Crow saw two paper cups stuck in a chain-link fence. One inside the other, they were both decorated with the blue key frieze of a Greek deli. It is impossible to overstate the importance of Greek delis, diners, and restaurants in Crow's epicurean pantheon. He remembered the remnants of a souvlaki in Astoria, an unfinished grilled sea bass in Sheepshead Bay, sidewalk cuisine suited to his temperament as a bird of the people, not refined or overly sophisticated. Honest and substantial. But the two cups incited more than memory. Were they put there both at once, or did one follow the other, from two different hands, a gesture of recognition, an act of solidarity, a concatenation beyond chance? Hardly the residue of chance. He knew by now that chance only reflects a lack of knowledge about the mechanisms that control our fate. In other words, this felt like a sign.

Crow studied the cups. They were festooned with symbols: a steaming cup, a temple, an amphora, a discus thrower, and the words: "We are happy to serve you." In the past, Crow treated them as generic decoration, clichés, stereotypes. But now he wasn't so sure. He had heard somewhere that the classics, so called, were under siege. Nobody read them. They had gone the way of foretelling by auguries and entrails. Homer? A mere name, a footnote to baseball discussions about steroids. Oedipus? A discredited patriarchal theory used to manufacture guilt. (Crow was not at all sure that he hadn't had sex with his mother; it would have happened so fast he might not have been able to make a positive ID.) But perhaps there was another order of knowledge contained in the ancient stories, in the labyrinths, one-eyed monsters, waxwings, and oracles. So the paper cups suggested.

Oracles: voices inspired from a cave of vapors, speaking in riddles that must come true. Knowledge of the future—for those who could parse this strange power of speech. Crow was no linguist, but he needed to know. Now that his eyes were opened.

Without having to look, he saw objects intentionally stuck in fences everywhere: beer cans, pieces of tree bark, cups of all sorts, rolled up newspapers, padlocks (hanging would be more accurate, like decorations on a holiday tree), tennis shoes, toy handguns (or were they toys?), bunches of flowers, both vegetable and plastic, stuffed animals, sunglasses—a panoply of overproduced earthly things suspended there. Not to mention stapled posters proclaiming every possible event or invitation: GhostFace Killah, Trump 2050, Call Sister Gertrude—She see your future what you got in your past.

What could it all mean?

One day, at the outskirts of the city, he was sitting on just such a fence trying to understand why a vacuum-cleaner hose had been hung there like a serpent when he noticed a pair of cowbirds huddled together on a nearby gate. Not several, a pair, a doubling, some sort of mirror effect. Twins? Crow checked that train of thought before it got far out of the station. In any case, they were out of their element, which is why they stuck out. They must have come from the burbs or way out in Jersey. The gate, too, had a plastic decoration, a sign that said, "No flyers. Nada. Never. Nohow." Hmmm. Crow never thought of cowbirds as flyers, more like interlopers. They were a scourge, lazy and mendacious, dropping their kids in other birds' nests and bugging off. The kids never seemed to learn from that and simply went on repeating their parents' offenses. Crow had no use for them, but they seemed to be talking about him, whispering in secret. He went over. They shut up immediately.

"Nice day for something. Haven't seen you around here before. Just visiting?" was all Crow had to say. He decided to cut to the chase. "I saw you talking about me. I'm not being self-centered. I just want to know why."

The cowbirds looked at each other as if asking, Well, should we tell him? Watching them, Crow realized he had seen them before, when he first noticed those two paper coffee cups in the fence. The fact that there were two cups now seemed intentional on a different level, maybe crucial. "I'm not leaving until you tell me."

There was more fluttering. One of them said, "We are happy to serve you in this regard. Our only hesitation is our reputation. We were just trying to decide if you would believe us, or whether you would think it was the liar's paradox." Put off by their weird formality, disconcerted by a phrase echoing a coffee cup, Crow tried to recall what the paradox was, something about being in a country of liars in which someone told you everyone was a liar. It couldn't be true, and it couldn't be false.

"You've been following me. Out with it. I'll have to take a chance with logical dead ends."

"Following you?" they said simultaneously. "Perhaps it's you who has been following us, but at a great distance. You wouldn't be the first creature blind to its own motives."

The two huddled for a moment, looking worried. Then once again answered together, in one voice. "Hasn't it struck you how easily and often you find the thing you are looking for? Everywhere. To be honest (there's that paradox again), we have been following you. Following what you do. Because we wanted to know why you keep putting these things into the holes of the chain-link fence. So many of us want to know. More and more every day."

Crow looked at them in astonishment. The plea, the indictment, seemed to reach him from a long way off, like the sound of a voice coming from a cave of vapors or the clouds in the sky. Could it be that he was the one, the one who had been creating this landscape of random precision, these collisions of chance and necessity? Or at least he had been ordained to discern what all others missed. He thought in a newly revealed light, like the blown-out image from an on-camera flash, of the fence. Of course, the fence! The key to everything! Object and metaphor, a regular structure of suspension for all the apparently haphazard things and experiences in the universe, a vast, unending lattice uniting even birds not of the same feather, not to mention duplicated gestures from separate moments—two cups, one inside the other. Reality unveiled, and his own destiny disclosed.

In that instant, Crow sensed himself whole and complete, a bicameral mind rescued at last from its schizophrenic division. In this new level of consciousness, all distant corners could be linked. The networks could not be explained to the unprepared, but he could bare for others their menacing splendor. All around him in the air, he could sense waves of digital communication. Nearby the wires of antiquated landlines hummed as if they were newly installed. Satellites traveled above the stratosphere, and drones circled overhead. Crow tracked them all, as if they were tied by infinitesimally thin wires and all to him, through him. We are happy to serve you. Crow the ultimate server, of unlimited storage capacity, the recipient of all data dumps, existed to connect the dots.

The patterns were potentially dazzling. The Greek key was a meandering river, a wrestler's grip, a design for a labyrinth. Its origins obviously Egyptian, as with all things ostensibly Attic. Who could deny the sect of the Ibis, operating down through time, its members the secret elect and every pyramid its symbol? Crow had heard of the Triangle Offense and its incredible success in the professional arena. He had once seen a picture of Phil Jackson and recognized the deep legacy of long-legged birds, the intersection of avian and human evolution. It must have begun long before the NBA, in the Nile delta. Someone once told him of a book in which a woman's black hair was described as dividing her face with the sharp line and sheen of a crow's wing. Perhaps a new race was emerging, with Brandon Lee as its avatar. Who believed anything they saw from Hollywood or even anything they read in a book? But he suspected everything came from Egypt. He knew there were birds that changed their feathers so many times they didn't know what they looked like. They passed back and forth among the two worlds as easily as smoke. They could be pets, parakeets, or vultures. The Merlin bird app had been hacked to identify species that never existed and cover the Egyptian tracks. There was nothing they didn't know and nothing they wouldn't do.

Let others explicate the apparent contradictions. Let others do the math and trace the lattice. Crow need only open the door of disparate phenomena—pizza parlors and pedophiles, mystic pyramids and Mozart operas, hand-delivered cash and Barak Obama's birth certificate—and a multitude would spin the theories and deliver the instructions. AI was only a sideshow to the expanding domain of artificial life. Artificial to whom (or what)? Two forms of life could co-exist only if there were two separate universes, and Crow had witnessed their collision in the accidents that were not accidental. There could be only one outcome, one final solution. Crow had no vision of a shining future, no agenda of salvation. Crow held out the satisfaction of knowingness and the lure of suspicion.

Crow cawed the questions: What is TikTok? Spying tool? Who created it? Who really created it? Why were Cairo street views taken down? Focus on his wife. Reread all dumps. Future answers the past. News unlocks maps. Check the autopsy. Look for the amputated wings. All faces are masks. All plumage is false. Expand your thinking. Expand your thinking.

A mere bird, Crow was legion. He took dominion everywhere. His name was Qrow.

Don't you think Crow would have eaten if he could have found a food that he liked? He was no hunger artist, and he used to say the world would always provide, but lately all that food seemed poisoned. That was because, against everything people thought and said about him, Crow chose to take sides in a shooting war. He sided with the victims.

There were three of them, a mother and two daughters, lying on a sidewalk, along a street, in a city once whole now littered with debris. As if it had been the contents of a pocket turned inside out and shaken. As if God, if there were such a thing, had stopped paying attention to the creation and allowed it to unravel. A bicycle lay nearby and a school backpack. Blood bloomed into black on all three in an identical place below the shoulder, as if what had happened to each had happened at the same time in exactly the same way.. Crow expected company at this ceremony, but the incredible concussions of heavy weapons must have knocked the magpies out of the sky and flattened even the mangiest of dogs in this starving place. Crow, too, had been floored but got himself up to view the devastation because he could, and that is, historically, what he did. What survivors do—survey devastation that he did not make. No need to feel remorse, Crow, it wasn't your fault. Just like those planes that fall out of the sky taking everyone on board with them. Crow wanted to say to them, even the pilots, you're not guilty. Dead but not guilty.

Not guilty. Or was there some other calculus by which everyone had it coming, even in the human world, where justice was often spoken about? Justice was in Crow's bones like a genetic memory he would never purge, indelible pre-images that seemed to say he was wedded to horror and could not live without its opportunities, its cycles of retribution and revenge, its tableaus staged just for him and incomplete until he arrived. Justice needed its opposite. How did Crow know that men were not broken by the wheel but on it? The wheel had not been used for torture in five hundred years, yet Crow remembered that you tied someone to it, then broke every bone you could find, then went on from there with whatever other depredation seemed to fit the mood—burning, disemboweling, flaying. Then you left remains as an *aide memoire*. Likewise, the gibbet. Likewise, the cross and the gallows. Likewise, the highway bridge, the city ramparts, the execution board where death by a thousand cuts might take all day. In the old days, the remnants of justice left a fertile field for his kind, and they thrived. Crow finally understood how the knowledge of retribution and martyrdom was bequeathed to him. It was in his bones.

So the three on the sidewalk could not help being familiar. Three identical wounds, three sudden unsought conclusions. He'd seen it all before. But something had happened. Death that was once so specific, as if its decisions were always particular, had lost interest in itself. It had become narcoleptic. And because in modern war killing was now unnecessary, it was all the more comprehensive. Kill them all because it was easier than killing individually, and they did. There is no such thing as a fought war, Crow thought, and no warriors, only killing without consequence. When had it started to go wrong? When had the little birds stopped coming?

To repeat for the hundredth time, Crow was an indifferent student of history, but he combed through a few scraps. For four years, the Italians and Austrians fought in the Dolomites, mountains jagged as dogs' teeth, to move a border back and forth eighteen feet. So, absurdity became the rule. But even then, they enjoyed the game, more deadly from avalanches than arms. By the time of the Dresden experiment, busy strategists had devised a plan to make sure fires could never be put out by killing anyone who tried to. Crow liked to think that there must have been cows grazing on the distant hills overlooking the Elbe, watching the eruptions of the expanding inferno zone with indifference. Or maybe they even liked the light show, but there was too much chewing to be done, and the smoke was a distraction. Probably a lot of birds managed to make it out to the suburbs. He knew that animals from the zoo in Berlin had wandered the streets at the downfall of the thousand-year Re-ich, free at last to starve like the rest of the survivors.

How long does it take to make a moonscape of a city? Or rather, how level can you make it? Crow didn't speak Japanese, but he knew the answer to both. The time approached zero, and the devastation approached infinity. It was the weapon to end all wars, the weapon no one would dare use. Except they did, if only to show why it shouldn't, which served as an imperative to use it again. He thought again of something the thrush had told him in Medellin: "If we had hands and feet, we could take over the world." Maybe he should have paid attention.

In his mind's eye, Crow sought to glut himself on scenes of horror, like the days of the old masters, who painted so well they could deceive even a clever crow with their beheadings and happy martyrdoms. Each saintly victim faithfully rendered, their agonies accepted and redeemed. But there were none in the art of Crow's time. There were only mountains of lugubrious, shadowless dead. Furniture victims, wallpaper victims, incongruous as piles of gold teeth or salvaged shoes. Invisible victims, whose only evidence were shadows etched on vestigial walls by a nuclear sun. There was poison in everything, but you could not see it. There was nothing that couldn't be expunged, dispatched into nonbeing never to return even in dreams.

Unable to take his mind's eye off these pictures of nothing, Crow realized they really were nothing. There was nothing in them. There were no beings. That was the riddle he was trying to plumb—and Crow hated riddles—as he looked and looked again at the three in the street. He had always thought, living or dead, these were beings just like him. They were there—here— the same way he was. But they weren't. They had been emptied out as mechanically as if they, too, had been atomized on an atoll. Still, someone had had to shoot them so surgically. For an instant it had to have been personal. But Crow realized that no one had done it. Whoever had pulled the trigger (did guns even need triggers anymore?) was not a being either but someone already nothing and so was perfect to empty out being from other beings and make them nothing. Nothing making more of itself.

Crow moved up closer to the three bodies. He thought if he stayed, if he would be a witness, first the mother would rise, and then her two daughters. These were only flesh wounds, after all. She would straighten her skirt, brush the little ones off, and they would run like hell for the nearest patch of shelter.

Or would they howl and incant devastating spells?

He watched them stiffen. Why are you still here, Crow? What are you waiting for? Do you think you can provide some remnant or memory of what disappears when a being finally disappears? Do you think you can be a reservoir of regret in the world, maybe the last reservoir? The tanks are coming. Cleaning up. Leveling down. On the other hand, not to worry. You don't even register. You can be the last, just like they always say, because nobody cares about you, and you can never speak what you know.

But Crow had no intention of waiting around, no interest in casting his shadow over the non-returning dead and the furrowed face of the Earth. No interest in pretending that all the deadly hardware didn't faze him. He knew that they who would murder these innocents would murder him. The contents of a school backpack, Hello Kitty it said, were scattered on the ground. There was blood on the strangely expressionless emoji. Hello Kitty, goodbye. Crow saw a blue colored pencil and picked it up in his beak. He lifted off and headed he didn't know exactly where, anywhere he might never see human beings again.

29. Groundhog Day

(in memory of Paul Celan)

Crow went walking in the mountains, or if not exactly the mountains, a place high up, in a field of rampion, clover, and lupines. A place where you feel free. Crow had walked a long way—why this choice to be earth-bound? No obvious answer, something about change for the sake of change or exercise of parts little used. Crow noticed the silence. He noticed how the land rolled and folded in a contour that shaped his thoughts down here. Walking thoughts, not flying thoughts.

A groundhog poked through the outline of the landscape, broke the surface and entered the realm Crow knew, shaking loose clots of earth from its muzzle. Crow saw him/her/it and thought: The opposite of going down is not coming up, it is *emerging*. The groundhog saw Crow, waited until he passed, then followed him. They walked on, individually and together. Crow was silent. The groundhog was silent, respecting Crow's silence. The two were silent together, traveling over the contours of a planet they couldn't see.

"You've come a long way," said Crow. The silence was partially broken by his voice.

"You've come a longer way," said the groundhog, "since you don't have to burrow through the sky."

Now the silence was completely broken. Silence does not ask to be filled until it is broken. "Where have you come from?" Crow asked.

"From going to and fro in the Earth, where it was quiet and

safe, putting my face up against the walls of soil and loam, seeing it feelingly. You?"

"From walking up and down on it, occasionally sailing above it, for a time." Crow thought for a minute, trying to work it out. "We've both come a ways to meet here, you from one realm, your face covered with dirt, me from another, my wings shiny, but neither one of us exactly finding each other. Because neither one of us was really looking."

The groundhog objected. "I had to have been looking or I would not have known to emerge just here and now. I don't like the light. My eyes aren't used to it."

"I just mean you weren't looking for *me*," answered Crow. "I wasn't looking for you. And yet . . ."

They both stopped at the same time, or perhaps Crow stopped first, and the groundhog felt an imperative to do the same. They could both smell a green smell, and the scent of valerian and lilies of the valley. Groundhog put his face in the dirt, feeling the temptation to go back under, into the thick confinement where home is everywhere. Crow looked up, sensing stratocumulus and feeling the temptation to get off his feet, get airborne again, into a different and familiar idiom with a thousand variants of the color blue.

"Look at us," said Crow, "barely moving, indecisive, neither here nor there."

They didn't actually look at each other, just kept thinking of earth and sky and the absolute impossibility of the realms being connected except through these two who met for no reason.

"If I look at you," said Crow, "I seem to see myself. Not as

I know me but as I am known—by everything else, you might say."

"And when I look at you, I seem to see nothing really, maybe because my eyes are so bad. But maybe I know you as you wish to be known, before life found you and, of course, after death takes you."

Crow had had a few moments when he truly stood outside of himself, without anything approaching ambition. At those moments, for all he knew, he was a groundhog. Or a rock, or a lupine, or a star.

The groundhog went on. "You know many things, Crow. That's how you are. And maybe why we've come together, I mean almost come together, in the mountains, I mean not exactly the mountains. I'm not very good with words. I have a hard time describing things. I don't know even one thing. But the thing I almost know is that there is no other world, a perfect world in which silence is golden and where we also understand what the other says. I almost know because once I came out of the ground for the first time. You have a nest, somewhere high up, but the dark earth is my nest. It is where I feel at home. In the light, the sudden light, I felt I was dissolving into nothing. And the sounds, Crow, the deafening sounds. But that was just the way it should have been since I had gone too far and gotten into a place where I didn't belong. But then I saw my shadow and realized I hadn't gotten anywhere. There was no threshold, and I hadn't crossed it, and I was right back where I started."

Groundhog's talk made Crow nervous. He moved in hurried starts, like a spider spooked from its web. Crow's thoughts dueled with each other like wizards, and his voice sounded like a bag full of sticks. "Then, so, this altitude I've been climbing up into while you were burrowing down confers nothing, conceals nothing, and confirms nothing. No beyond. I'm not asking, just thinking out loud, just repeating what you're saying."

"Maybe if you manage to get to the stars, some star, something so distant that its light hitting us means it's already dead and gone. But then what? Even there you would probably see your shadow, the way I saw mine, and always see mine. You would say, 'It's me again.'"

"Hah," Crow laughed mirthlessly (if that's the expression for a laugh that isn't a laugh). "Then what is the point of all this? The rampion and lilies of the valley and the valerian, which is purple, and the lilies are small and white? Your burrowing and my flying and all this walking and talking, independently and together, and meeting without exactly meeting?"

"Someone observing us would think I knew everything and you knew nothing, Crow, when the exact opposite is true. Looking around, here, above ground in the mountains that aren't quite, with my terrible eyesight, the only thing I can say is that it looks like a beautiful day, and it almost makes me feel good to be alive."

Crow kept walking, more agitated than ever. "I wouldn't go that far," he said. What he meant was: I would almost go that far. What he really meant was: We're ending where we should be beginning. What he finally managed to say was: "I understand everything you say except the word *alive*."

30. Crow in Extremis

At the last moment, Crow found his ironic pedantry and picturesque erudition had deserted him. Embroidering experience with illusions and fantasies was more than he could manage. You could say he was almost relieved. You could say he was almost happy.

Nightmare of a long bus trip in an unfamiliar but recollected country: Denmark?

Nightmare of loose teeth

Nightmare of a complicated house to which you keep returning

Nightmare of resurrected mother—silent

Nightmare of resurrected brother—silent

Nightmare of polite refusal—still not being impressive enough

Nightmare of unconsummated sex

Nightmare of falling

Nightmare of appearing in church with no pants

Nightmare of wallpaper

Nightmare of rising water in the kitchen

Nightmare of the unprepared speech

Nightmare of uncontrolled anger

Nightmare of unremembered chums

Nightmare of exposure in front of children

Nightmare of a humid room with radiator

Nightmare of multiple cigarettes

Nightmare of forgotten examinations

Nightmare of previous nightmares

Nightmare of waking up into another dream, and waking up again

Postscript

The following thanks are due to all those who read Crow at an early stage and heard his voice:

Rachel Klein, without whom . . .

Charles Traub, Christopher James, Phong Bui, Dan Estabrook, Doug Campbell, Donald Alberti, Heidi Owsley, Maria Consagra, Nick Schiff, Jose Falconi, Grey Crawford, Barry Munger, Steel Stillman, Barry Schwabsky, Mariana Alzamora, Mary Ellen Trahan, and John Tillman

Lyle Rexer holds two degrees from Columbia University and was a Rhodes Scholar at Merton College, Oxford University. He is the author of many books, including *How to Look at Outsider Art* (2005), *The Edge of Vision: The Rise of Abstraction in Photography* (2009), for which he was awarded a grant from the Creative Capital/Andy Warhol Foundation, and *The Critical Eye: 15 Pictures to Understand Photography* (2019). He has published hundreds of catalogue essays, reviews, and articles on art, photography, and contemporary literature and contributed to such publications as *The New York Times*, *Art in America*, *Aperture*, *BOMB*, *Harper's*, and the *Brooklyn Rail*. As a curator, he has organized exhibitions in the United States and internationally and has lectured at many institutions, including the Metropolitan Museum of Art, The Whitney Museum of American Art and Yale University.